Publish or perish

A mystery editor is found slumped across her desk, with a rejection note stapled to her sleeve and a bullet hole through her heart—for the second time. Does the murder have a personal motive, or is it just a frustrated writer who can't deal with rejection? The New York City police captain vetoes an investigation of thousands of suspects, so Detective Brian Skiles and editor Anne Baker must set a deadly trap to catch the killer, and to prove the pen is mightier than the sword.

The Last Page

by Bob Fenster

A mystery from Perseverance Press
Menlo Park, California

Art direction by Gary Page/Merit Media.
Photography by Rob Egashira/Fabrizio Camera Graphics.
Portraits of mystery writers © Frank Hamilton and Brad Foster, courtesy of artists and Bob Napier, *Mystery & Detective Monthly.*
Typography by Jim Cook/Book Design & Typography.

Published by
Perseverance Press
P.O. Box 384
Menlo Park, California 94026

Manufactured in the United States of America.

This book is printed on acid-free paper.

1 2 3 — 91 90 89

Library of Congress Catalog Card Number 88-64025.

ISBN 0-9602676-8-9

This novel is a work of fiction. Any resemblance to real situations or to actual people, living or dead, is completely coincidental.

To my wife, Anne Bothwell,
who knows a few things about first and
last pages and the journey between.

The Last Page

Chapter 1

"You want the truth?" Jessica Brody asked.

"That's why I'm here."

As an editor, Jessica knew it was unprofessional to tell bad writers the truth about their books. But Tuesday had been worse than Monday, and Monday had been terrible.

Her top author was threatening to jump to a rival publisher. Her boss had accused her of spending too much money on books that weren't bringing in enough. And her ulcers had turned against her again.

At a time like this, Jessica thought, there was no point in taking it all out on yourself. Better to take it out on someone else. Someone like a pushy, no-talent writer, like the one who sat across the desk from her two hours after the office had closed, wasting Jessica's precious overtime.

"The truth is," Jessica said, "your book stinks. Thousands of mystery novels cross my desk each year, and yours is the worst. I'd never publish it. Your characters are flat, the story is stupid, and you type lousy too. Do some tree a favor and don't write any more. Nothing personal, you understand."

There, now she felt better. Jessica slipped the manuscript back into its box and handed it across the desk. Then she saw the gun.

That explains the gloves, she thought.

Before she could think anything else, the gun fired. The force of the bullet slammed Jessica backwards. She bounced off the wall and fell dead across her desk, her head landing in the out-box.

The killer took out a piece of paper and stapled it to the sleeve of Jessica's blouse. Then the killer picked up the manuscript and left.

Chapter 2

BRIAN SKILES WAS LATE for the murder. He had been at a movie, taking in a revival of Fellini's *Amarcord* for the fifth time. Brian loved films, but only those that weren't about New York City or crime.

After the movie, he phoned the desk because he was working an open case for Captain Stark. When the captain was jumpy, it was advisable not to be out of touch for too long. The deskman told Brian about the murder, that Captain Stark wanted him at the publishing offices of Peters and Pryor on 52nd off Fifth ASAP.

It was after midnight when Brian showed his badge to the uniformed officer outside the door and stepped into the office.

The first thing Brian saw was the victim, pitched head-first across the only desk in the room. Behind that desk were two bookcases filled with dictionaries, thesauruses, and other reference books.

There were three Edward Hopper prints on the walls, a lunch counter and two office scenes. Lining the other three walls were shelves holding hundreds of cardboard boxes. Brian knew the boxes contained book manuscripts sent in by people who wanted to become writers but couldn't until an editor said they could. He had seen hundreds of similar boxes in the first editor's office.

Brian opened his overcoat and rubbed his face, which was raw from the late February cold spell. He stepped further into the office and checked on the activity.

A photographer from the police lab was taking Polaroids of everything in sight. Two tech assistants were dusting for prints, but it didn't look like they were going to find any. People who planned murders didn't leave prints, hadn't for years. TV had taught them not to.

The medical examiner stood beside the desk smoking, shaking his head, although it wasn't clear what he was shaking it about. He didn't have much to do until the tech crew was through because the woman had been shot and she'd died of it, unless an autopsy proved differently. He knocked the ash from his cigarette into his jacket pocket and shook his head again. A philosopher, Brian thought.

Across the desk from the medical examiner, Detective Al Viso stood motionless, his hands jammed into overcoat pockets, his pale gray eyes shifting from one object on the desk to the next, searching for a clue that would point him in a direction.

In the far corner of the room, Captain Stark and Sergeant Cranston were talking to a cleaning woman. She'd probably found the body, Brian thought. Cleaning women were always finding bodies. Tough job.

Brian walked over to Al Viso. "Who's the vic? Another editor?"

"Jessica Brody," Al said, his gaze continuing steadily from object to object. "Mystery editor for this company, Peters and Pryor. Took one shot to the heart sometime earlier tonight. Dr. Dickens over there figures three, maybe four hours ago, but he's not ready to go on record yet. Cleaning woman found her."

"Killer leave another note?"

"Take a look for yourself." Al grabbed the photographer's arm. "You finished yet?"

The photographer, who had taken pictures of the victim from the front, back, and both sides, was now up on a chair trying for an overhead. "Whatever," he said.

Brian saw the paper stapled to Jessica Brody's shirt sleeve. He lifted her arm and read the note:

"We regret to inform you," the note said, "that your life does not meet our current needs. We wish you better luck elsewhere."

"Same note as the first time?" the photographer asked.

"Exactly." Brian gently put the arm back on the desk. Funny, he thought, how careful we are with people after it's too late to do them any good.

"I missed that one," the photographer said. "I was shooting my cousin's wedding. Cheap bastard. Between murders and weddings, I'll take murders anytime. At least the relatives don't bug you for free prints."

"I don't like this one, Brian," Al Viso said. "The guy's got a weird sense of humor."

"The killer or the photographer?" Brian asked. "Any witnesses?"

"Nope. The vic was working late, only one here. No sign of a break-in. The killer either had a key or Ms. Brody let him in herself."

"We're through," one of the tech assistants announced. Al went over to confer with him as the medical examiner rubbed out the cigarette on his notebook and dropped the butt into his pocket. Then he moved in on the body.

Brian crossed the room to the captain, as Sergeant Cranston led the cleaning woman to the door. One of the uniformed officers would see her out of the building; getting through the rest of the city would be up to her.

"Don't ask," Captain Stark told Brian. "She didn't see anything, didn't hear anything, doesn't know anything. She found the body at ten and called nine-one-one."

A short man in an overcoat with a fur collar stepped into the office doorway, looked at Jessica Brody and said, "Oh, good Lord."

"That would be Mr. Peters or Mr. Pryor," Stark said. He signaled to Cranston and Viso, who converged on the man.

"Same rejection note as the first victim," Brian said.

"You're not going to bring up that stupid theory again?" Stark asked. "I hate stupid theories, and I'm not crazy about the people who bring them up either."

Captain Stark rubbed his forehead, as if pained by all the stupid theories he had been forced to endure in his career. Stark fingered the scar, as thin and long as a worry line, that ran across his forehead and into his silver temples. Brian had been there when the tall junkie who didn't want to be arrested slashed Stark with a razor. Plastic surgery had covered all but the faintest scar, but it had not healed the wound.

"One thing about my theory," Brian said. "It fits. Two mystery editors shot in their offices late at night. Each vic gets pinned with a rejection note. 'We reject your life.' It's like the notes writers get when their books are rejected."

Stark lit a cigarette, dropping the match on the floor, and blew smoke up into Brian's face. Stark was the perfect six-footer, with a large, handsome face, cleft chin and wide shoulders. Only problem was he wasn't six feet; he stood five-foot-nine. While that may have been the national average, it made life tough for a cop who thought of himself as on the way up.

Of course, if the captain had been taller, the junkie's razor would have cut lower. But Stark didn't see his stature as good fortune. Neither did the junkie, for that matter, whom Stark shot four times but who still didn't die, although he often wished he had.

"The note was meant to throw us off track," Stark said, flicking ashes onto the office rug. "Which it has obviously done with you."

"Unless I'm right," Brian said.

Stark shook his massive head. "We do not have a frustrated writer running around New York City killing editors who reject his book. People don't do that."

"What if they do?"

"They don't. And do you know why they don't? Because I already have a couple of hundred legitimate suspects who knew both editors, worked with them, maybe slept with them. What I don't need is another twenty thousand suspects I don't have any idea who they are. Now get out of here. Go knock on some doors. Make yourself generally useful."

"Make a guy a captain and he starts to act like he knows something," Brian said. "Someone might forget you and I were partners once."

"I already have," Stark said. "That's the secret of my success. That, and I don't look for impossible solutions to simple murders."

"Simple, huh? The only thing simple here is . . ."

"Come on, Brian." Al Viso pulled Brian away. "I need your help."

Sergeant Cranston hurried over after Al. "I spoke to the victim's boss," he said. "Mr. Peters was at a party at his apartment all evening, and his partner, a Mr. Pryor, was there too. He can't think of who would want to murder Ms. Brody. But I have obtained a list of current employees of the firm."

"Get some men over there to question them," Stark said, glaring after Brian.

"It's one in the morning."

"Good, check for cold sheets. Then get to her friends, lovers, relatives and anyone else who would want to kill her. I want this case solved before someone else comes up with more stupid theories. And what is that man doing on the phone?" He pointed to the short man with the fur collar who was using the phone on Jessica Brody's desk.

"That's Mr. Peters, the boss here," Cranston said.

"I know that," Stark said. "Why is he talking into a piece of evidence?"

"I think he's calling around," Cranston said, "looking for a new editor."

Al Viso walked Brian to the door. "When are you going to learn?" he asked, keeping his grip on Brian's arm. "You've got enough trouble."

Brian had drawn the initial assignment on the first murder, a month ago. But when he hadn't solved it after three days, Captain Stark had moved in, relabeling the case a major crime, a category of murder that meant important people cared about having it solved. People like influential publishers and their society contacts. If the captain solved the case, he got the favorable attention of people who could make significant political paybacks.

Stark also knew that it couldn't hurt to have the second biggest book publisher in the country owe him a favor, that at some time in his career there might be an autobiography of a cop published and it might even be titled *Commissioner* the way another successful politician's book had been titled *Mayor.*

Taking over the first murder case was a risky move, though, because if the captain didn't solve it, all the important people he was trying to please would not be pleased. Now a second murder, probably related, although he could hope they weren't, had complicated everything and raised the stakes.

That's why Captain Stark kept Brian Skiles assigned to the case, doing semi-independent parts of the investigation. If the case did prove unsolvable, Stark would have someone around to pass as much of the blame to as possible.

Al Viso understood that situation. Brian Skiles did too. He just didn't care.

"None of that stuff is important," he told Al. "If I'm right, then this isn't the last book killing. Somewhere out there, a crazy writer is waiting for his book to be rejected a third time so he can kill again. And somewhere, an editor is about to do it to him."

Chapter 3

ANNE BAKER RAN OFF a fresh batch of rejection slips on the copy machine and sat down to tackle her slush pile. Skimming through the manuscripts, she stuffed rejection slips into the envelopes with a speed that other editors envied.

When a tall, bland-looking man entered her office, Anne knew what he was right away. "No writers," she said. "I never see writers."

Anne turned back to the manuscript on her desk, hoping he would take the hint. She saw a flash of something metallic.

"Detective Brian Skiles," the man said. "New York City Police Department."

Anne looked up wearily. The man held some kind of badge out toward her. "That line may have gotten you past the front desk," she said. "But I've been around. I've had writers pretend to be plumbers, building inspectors, fire marshals. One writer claimed to be my cousin, and I don't have cousins."

"I'm not a writer. I'm a cop."

"If there's one thing I hate worse than writers pretending to be cops," Anne said, "it's cops pretending to be writers."

"Look, I don't write books. I don't even read books."

"Not impressed," Anne said. "Most writers never read anything but their contracts. Doesn't stop them from writing. That's my job."

"I'm not . . ."

"And I never buy books from people who try to sell me books," Anne said. "If you want to be a writer, go away and write. Simple, isn't it?"

"Don't you ever stop talking long enough to . . ."

"Certainly not. That only gives the opposition a chance to move in. Look, I hate to be rude, but get out of my office. Actually, I don't hate it that much."

Brian watched her as she talked, fascinated by how long she was: thin face, long body, arms and fingers long and thin.

"Lady," he said, "do I have to arrest you to get you to shut up for a minute?"

"Wouldn't work. I know my rights. Anything I say will be used against me. So I say, get out. Now use it against me."

Long and odd, too, Brian thought. This Anne Baker had organized herself to keep preparations to a minimum: short, straight hair, no make-up, no jewelry at ears, neck, wrists or fingers.

Despite her attempts at non-adornment, the total effect was exotic, daring. Her skin was pale, milky against her cream-colored blouse and brown skirt. The top button of her blouse was open, showing off the length of her neck.

Her brown hair was two shades lighter than her dark eyes, two splashes of color on a long, pale rider. With looks like that, Brian thought, too bad this was business. Then again, perhaps it was better that this was business.

"This has nothing to do with books," Brian said.

"I have hundreds of manuscripts to reject," Anne said. "All of them from would-be writers who are waiting anxiously for me to crush their dreams."

"One of them may be a killer."

"Perhaps all of them are," Anne said. "They're certainly not writers."

"Did you know Jessica Brody?" Brian asked. "Senior mystery editor at Peters and Pryor."

"Only to sneer at."

"She was murdered in her office last night. No witnesses, no fingerprints. Only one clue, a note pinned to the victim."

Maybe he really is a cop, Anne thought, looking at the man closely for the first time. He wasn't bland exactly; he was average. With medium brown hair cut to an average length, a handsome face but not too handsome, well-built but not bulky, tall but not basketball tall.

He wore a nondescript gray suit, white shirt, and blue tie, his clothes neither cheap nor expensive. He looked like he had added up every businessman in Manhattan and made himself up in their average image. There was nothing distinctive about the man. Except for his eyes, which were too steady and watched too much.

Brian held out a copy of the note they had found stapled to Jessica Brody's sleeve. Anne took the paper and read it.

"It's like a rejection slip," she said, "the kind we send to writers. Did it come from the killer?"

"Yes. I believe the format of the rejection slip is similar at every publishing house?"

"The words may change, but the message is always the same," Anne said. "We try to be polite about it. After all, we may not want to buy their books, but we do want them to buy ours. Are you suggesting that whoever killed Jessica Brody is a frustrated writer?"

"That's what I believe."

"That's insane."

"That's what my captain believes."

"If rejected writers killed the editors who reject them," Anne said, "there wouldn't be any editors left."

"Jessica Brody wasn't the first," Brian said. "You remember Amy Johnson, the mystery editor from Joss House?"

"She was murdered a month ago. But everyone said her husband did it."

"Including the captain. But no one's been able to prove it."

"How do the two murders connect?"

"Both editors were killed in their offices while working alone at night."

"All editors work nights. It's the only time we can get any actual editing done." Anne frequently worked at night alone in her office. But there was a guard in the lobby and the front door was locked and, besides, no one had any reason to kill her. She had been rejecting people for years; that was her job. People don't get killed for doing their jobs. Maybe cops did, but normal people didn't.

"They were both shot by the same gun," Brian continued, "and they . . ."

"Were given the same rejection note?"

"Yes, identical."

"What does this have to do with me?"

"I think the killer will strike again."

"Why?"

"The rejection notes he left with the bodies, they were copies."

"A form letter," Anne said. "We use them because we send out thousands a year."

"This killer also knows how to pick his editors," Brian said. "The two victims worked for the two biggest mystery publishers in the business."

"And I work for the third," Anne said. She looked quickly over to the door, as if the killer were about to burst through. "Which means I'm the next target."

Brian pointed to the pile of manuscripts on her desk. "The killer's book might be there right now."

"Waiting for me to reject it so he can kill me."

"I'm here to stop him."

"Hold that thought a moment," Anne said. She picked up the phone and punched two buttons. As it rang, she opened a desk drawer and tossed some papers into her briefcase.

"Is Brandon in?" Anne said into the phone. "It's Anne Baker down in mysteries. Then let me leave a message for him. When he gets back to the office, tell him it's been swell but I quit. Bye-bye." Anne hung up the phone and continued to pack her briefcase.

"You can't quit like that," Brian said.

"I've quit jobs because I didn't like the wallpaper. I guess I can quit to save my life."

"You don't understand," Brian said. "I'm going to catch this killer, and I need your help."

"I need your help too." Anne pointed to a carton of books on top of a credenza. "Dump out those books and hand me the box."

Brian ignored her request. "I won't let anything happen to you."

"That's what they all say." Anne dumped the books out herself and started sorting file folders into the box. "Then the lights grow dim and you hear a funny noise and you start walking backwards, and pretty soon you're dead. Not me, friend."

"Somewhere out there is a killer getting away with murder. We have to stop him."

"Why?"

"Because if we don't, no one will."

"Count me with them. I'm a book editor. I make fantasies real, and I can't do that if I'm dead. I hate to be obvious, but goodbye."

Chapter 4

BRIAN HUNG UP his holster and picked up a brush. He stared at the forest that covered the wall in his apartment.

Winter, he decided, was almost over. He had been painting the forest mural for ten months, putting the trees, the animals, the light through the changes of season. For two months, he had been working snow scenes. But soon the snow would melt, the birds reappear from the southeast corner and spring would complete the cycle. He dipped the brush in brown paint and started on the tail of the fox.

Tomorrow, he would go talk to the mystery editor at the fourth largest book publisher and make the same pitch he had tried on Anne Baker. If he got turned down there, he would go on to the fifth house, then the sixth. One way or another, he would get to an editor before the killer did.

The phone rang. He put down the brush. "Skiles."

"My name is Janice Merril," a woman said. "Barbara Aaron suggested I call you."

"Yes," Skiles said.

"I'm in town for a business meeting," Janice said. "I'd like to take you out for dinner tonight."

Brian looked at the mural, at the outline of the fox watching from a copse of pines. He shrugged; winter was in no hurry. "I'll meet you at the Golden Spike across from Lincoln Center in an hour."

"I'll make reservations," Janice said. "Barbara told me you were with the police."

"I'm a detective."

"Do me a favor; bring your gun. New York, you know."

Anne Baker was writing her third farewell letter to her third favorite author when Claire Deluthe came into the office. Claire was the romance editor at Everall Publishing and she dressed for the part. This evening, she wore lace, with the slightest hint of pink frosting in her blonde curls. "Working late again tonight?" she asked.

Anne hoped Claire would come close enough so she could spill something on her, but Claire stayed by the door. "You know how it is," Anne said. "It's either work late or meet the prince for dinner at Chez Madeline."

"I used to work late before I got an assistant," Claire said. "Maybe if *you* get your sales up, Brandon will get you an assistant. Although there's a rumor going round that you're quitting or got fired or something."

"I haven't made my rumor quota lately, that's all. If I were quitting, I wouldn't be working late."

"Some people work late so they don't have to go home. But I must run. I'm meeting Brandon for dinner. Be sure to shut off the lights when you leave. You're the last one here as usual."

"That was a great piece of veal," Janice Merril said, pushing away her plate. "Back in San Diego, all the veal comes surrounded by guavas and mangos."

"New York is a meat town." Brian smiled at Janice, who nodded. She was a big woman, neither plain nor pretty, wearing a business suit with a bow around her throat.

"I always think I'll be too nervous to eat in New York," she said, "but I always do."

"You're not crazy about the city, I take it?"

"I feel like a statistic here. Either something will happen to me so the crime-watchers can prove how dangerous New York is, or I'll escape harm so the tourist people can claim that it's not as dangerous as people say. Why do you live here?"

"I was raised here," Brian said. "It's in my blood."

Janice signaled the waiter. "Could we skip dessert? I have an executive session early tomorrow and then I have to catch a flight back."

"Sure, where are you staying?"

"Your place." Janice tossed a credit card on top of the bill. "My assistant sales manager has the room next to mine. If he heard us in there, he'd use it as a bargaining chip for his next performance review."

Anne was in the storage closet, filling a box with personal items, when the phone rang. It was the night guard, 20 floors below.

"You forgot to let me know you were working late again, Ms. Baker," he said.

"Sorry, Phil. I'll do it next time, I promise."

"Anyway, your sandwich is here. Want me to send the guy up?"

"Have him wait," she told the guard. "I'll come down and get it myself."

Janice Merril came back into the bedroom carrying a glass of water. Moonlight through the window caught her naked body the way a flashlight catches an animal in the night forest. She drank half the water, sat on the bed, and handed him the rest. She reached under the sheets.

"New York has one thing over San Diego," she said.

"And what would that be?" Brian asked.

"The sexual tension here is incredible. I've never been so primed. Back home it's, 'Would you prefer sex or another margarita?' Here you could do it fifty times a block."

"Or perhaps twice a night?"

"How about that?" Janice said. "You're a mind reader too."

Anne had finished cleaning out her desk. She'd typed all the letters she was going to write and left the few instructions that her successor would need. It was half past nine, but she was almost through. She went into the storage closet to collect a few copies of her favorite mysteries. That's when she heard the clubbing sound.

It came from somewhere down the hall outside her office. In the emptiness it sounded loud, like a club smashing against a wooden door.

"I get you," a man called. His voice had a foreign accent, and there was a touch of mad glee in it.

She looked around for a weapon. On the shelves were piles of manuscripts, galleys from the typesetter, paste-up boards, and page proofs.

Whack! The club again, from the hall, and the man's voice, "Now you die, little one."

She grabbed a book, a copy of *Death Goes Long* which was not one of her favorites but was 400 pages thick.

Through the smoked-glass window of her office door, she saw something, long and tubular like a pistol with a silencer. She stepped to the side and pressed her back against the wall.

Whack! Then a scratching sound against the door. She looked down, clutching the book over her head. A mouse scurried under the door and darted along the wall.

She screamed. The door flew open. A man charged inside, swinging something long and wicked, an axe, a club. She hit him with the book, whipping it at his head with her long arms.

He yelled and fell, dropping the broom. He looked up with terror in his eyes. She threatened him with the book. He backed away from her on the floor and started laughing.

"What do you want?" Anne asked.

The man rubbed his head. He was big and bony, with a long nose, wearing overalls and a woolen shirt. He shrugged. "What does any man want?" His accent was Polish, maybe Russian. "To be rich and make love to cheerleaders in long, white socks."

"Who are you?"

"Janitor. Good janitor, very."

"You didn't come here to kill me?" Anne kept the book cocked over her head.

"Not kill. Empty trash. Chase mouse, little Mickey."

"You're not the regular janitor."

"Temporary. Everyone temporary. That's life."

Anne had begun to relax. Now she was suspicious again. "You sound like a novelist pretending to be a janitor so you can sell me a book."

"America crazy country." The man stood up. "Django not novelist. Django last great unpublished Russian gypsy poet who suffers."

Anne backed away toward her desk. "Yes, I'm sure you do. We all suffer with poets."

Django followed her, swiping at the floor with his broom. "To you, great lady editor, I give amazing American once-in-a-lifetime chance. Publish poetry and Django is janitor no more."

"No poetry. No poets."

"I read." Django pulled some folded yellow papers from an overall pocket. "The tractors of my heart plough the fields of your eyes with love . . ."

"If there's one thing I've always admired about Russians," Anne said, "it's that most of them live eight thousand miles away."

Django threw down the broom. "Django cleans no more. Better I suffer. Come back, little Mickey. She is all yours."

As Django stormed from the office, Anne started laughing. She laughed until it turned to shivers of fear. She ran to her desk and picked up the phone.

Brian lay in his bed, watching Janice dress in the moonlight. "You could stay," he said, "another day, another night."

She looked in the mirror to tie the bow around her neck. "If I miss my plane, Bo will get upset."

"Your husband?"

"My parakeet."

The phone rang. Brian picked it up on the first ring. Janice sat on the bed to put on her shoes. "Skiles," Brian said.

"Anne Baker. Let's make a deal."

She sounded nervous. "Did something happen?" Brian asked.

"Yeah, I figured out how to make a killing from catching a killer. Meet me, tomorrow morning. My office."

Brian looked up as Janice headed for the door. She turned and waved at him. He nodded. "All right."

"Good. But don't wear a suit tomorrow. Switch to a corduroy jacket or a tweed."

"Why should I?"

"So you won't have to go home and change in the middle of the day," Anne said, and hung up.

Chapter 5

"WHAT'S WRONG WITH my gray suit?" Brian asked when he walked into Anne's office the next morning.

Anne looked at Skiles' corduroy jacket, brown pants, and white shirt. Still a crowd-melter, but at least the right crowd.

"Never mind your clothes for now," Anne said. "Let's talk about us."

"You've decided to help me trap the killer?" Brian sat down.

"I've decided that what we have here is a great book."

Brian stood up. "You don't seem to firmly grasp the concept that these murders are real. Real killer, real victims."

"Right, non-fiction," Anne said. "The way I look at it, we've got a best-seller here."

"What are you talking about? And do I want to know?"

"We catch the killer," Anne said, "fine. But we also write a book about it. Mystery editor and renegade cop trap mad killer. My company publishes the book, and I turn it into a best-seller. Can't miss."

"That's not for me. I catch killers. I don't do books."

"Think about the money, the movie rights," she said. "Think about *People* magazine."

Brian sighed. He liked looking at her, being close to her, the long, pale rider. But business was business. "I'm a cop," he said. "That's all I'm good at."

"So you'll be a rich cop. You can have your chauffeur drive the patrol car."

"No deal." Brian stood up and headed for the door.

"You need me," Anne said. "I don't need you. I'm the target, whether you're here or not."

Brian turned back and looked at her. So unadorned and so

exotic. If the killer got her, the mortician would put more make-up on her than she wore now.

"You don't know anything about catching killers," he said.

"I'm a mystery editor. I've solved more murders than you have."

She would be difficult to work with. But then solving a murder was either very easy or very hard, fast or too slow. "You write the book," he said. "I'll catch the killer."

"Then we have a deal?"

"Deal." Brian walked over to the desk and extended his hand. She looked at his hand as if checking it for weapons and shook it briefly. She tossed a contract on the desk.

"Sign this." As Brian looked the contract over, she picked up the phone and punched two numbers. "Is Brandon back from his trip yet? Well, when he does, tell him I unquit. I'm back on the job."

When she hung up, Brian pointed at the contract. "I can't make sense of this."

"You're not supposed to make sense of it," Anne said. "It's a book contract. Just sign it. Basically, it says if we sell a lot of books, you'll get rich but we'll get richer."

"Won't your boss worry about risking your life for a book?"

"You kidding? If he thought it would increase sales, he'd hire someone to shoot every author he has. Now first, we'll have to do something about you. You look too much like a cop."

"I am a cop."

"This is a high rumor business," Anne said. "If people around here find out you're a cop, everyone in the industry will know it by tomorrow and the writers will hear about it the day after that. We might as well put an ad in the *Times* book review section: Editor and cop looking for killer. Experience necessary."

"What do you suggest?"

"We'll have to tell my boss. That's okay. He forgets everything I tell him anyway. To everyone else, you'll be my new assistant editor. Which means you'll have to dress like one. Which means no more of those gray suits."

"What's wrong with that suit? It's what half the men in Manhattan wear every day. It helps me blend in."

"Blending is wonderful if you're a daiquiri. But editors are expected to display a little flair. Also, put some ink stains on your shirts. They're the scars of our profession. Plus, never go anywhere without two pens and a notebook in your pocket."

"I never do." Brian showed her his police notebook, thin cardboard.

"Wrong kind. Have one of mine." Anne gave him a thick, leather-covered notebook.

"A thin notebook says we don't have enough work to do, so someone will find more work to pile on. A thick notebook says we have so much work to do you don't want to ask us about it because we might waste your time telling you."

Brian put the new notebook in his jacket. "Am I ready now?"

"As soon as you learn how to talk like an editor."

"You mean proper English?"

"Certainly not. I mean shop talk. First, never talk books. But always talk editing."

"For example?"

"Let's say you're talking to one of the guys in the marketing department, so you talk sports."

"Like, 'Did you see the Mets' game last night?' "

"Yes, and he'll say, 'I knew Gooden was going to win.' "

"Right, your average sports talk."

"Right, only you say, 'And did you see that typo on the scoreboard in the bottom of the eighth? They can't even spell Cincinnati right.' That's editor talk."

"I get it. It's kind of like cop talk. We would say, 'You see that guy sitting behind third when Carter hit the foul ball? Looked like that pickpocket I put away in eighty-five.' But what do I say if someone should start talking to me about books?"

"Not likely to happen around here," Anne said. "But if it does, it will be another editor complaining about how some crazy writer is driving her insane. So you say, 'Writers, they're all like that.' And she'll realize that you know the score. Or if someone asks you about a book we're working on, simply say, 'It's a mystery to me, but we hope to save it in the editing.' Then they'll know you've been around."

"You think I can get away with it?"

"Sure you can. Editors come and editors go, and that's the way everyone will think of you."

"Then let's get to work." Brian indicated the pile of manuscripts on her desk. "I'll start by reading through your slush pile. See if any of them contain clues to the murders."

"Use that desk." Anne pointed to the only other desk in the room, which faced hers. "I'll get the rest." She went into the storage closet.

Brian took a long look around the room. Besides the two gray metal desks, there were four file cabinets and two book cases, with the storage closet in the wall opposite Anne's desk. On the other walls were photos of authors sitting at typewriters. Brian circled the room, reading the names on the photos: Dashiell Hammett, Raymond Chandler, Charlotte Armstrong, Kenneth Fearing, Richard Stark, Ed McBain, Joe Gores.

"All these your writers?" he called to Anne.

She laughed. "If they were, I'd be rich. Also older. These are the ones I like."

Anne came back pushing a cart piled high with a hundred manuscript boxes. She parked it next to his desk and handed him a stack of rejection slips, which explained that the book didn't meet their needs at this time, better luck elsewhere.

"As long as you're reading, drop a rejection slip in each one so I can have them mailed back."

"What should I do if I find a good book?"

"Faint. That's what I always do."

"How many books do you reject each year?" Brian took a look in the closet, where rows of gray metal shelves held piles of manuscripts waiting their turn.

"Nearly all of them," Anne said. "I publish seventy, eighty mystery novels a year. I receive thousands of manuscripts. You figure the odds any of them have of getting published. And remember that of the seventy I do publish, fifty of them come from established writers, the pros who churn them out year after year."

Brian paced the room. "That's too many suspects. We have to eliminate some, a few thousand at least. How many manuscripts do you have in-house right now?"

"Five, maybe six hundred."

"How do you manage so much reading?"

"When I have the budget for assistants, I let them screen the books. They'll find maybe a hundrd a year that are worth my real consideration. Out of that lot, I'll pick ten or twenty. The rest they put back in their self-addressed, stamped envelopes and ship back to all the would-be writers who will never become pros but won't stop trying, though whole forests could be saved if they did. If ecologists want to save trees, they should go after the amateur writers and leave the loggers alone."

"How do you keep up with so much reading when you don't have assistants?"

"Really bad books are bad from the beginning. So I don't have to read much to tell it's something I would never publish."

"How much of a book do you read?"

"Ten pages, five. Some you can tell by the first page, by the title or the cover letter. If the manuscript comes in a pink box with stars and hearts pasted all around the address, and they do, you can safely figure that you don't have the next Raymond Chandler on your hands."

"Must make it hard on the writers. They put in months writing hundreds of pages and you throw them back after ten."

"It's hard on us too." Anne's voice tightened in anger, the muscles standing out along her neck. "Every new editor tries to give each writer a fair chance," Anne said. "Reads the entire book, searching for genius in the rough. It usually takes about a day and a half to get cured of that notion. Cynicism sets in, and that's what makes you a professional. That's how you survive in this business. We're not very nice, I suppose. But some publishing houses won't even read unsolicited manuscripts, send them back unopened."

"Why?"

"Costs too much money, and it wears out a good editor to read so many bad books. Erodes your sense of quality. Why should I read a thousand books, knowing I'm only going to publish one of them? It's crazy, like watching TV all day just to see one good show. I may miss a good book now and then, but I'm also going to save my company a lot of money and myself a lot of stress."

"Tough business."

"Tough for them, tough for us," Anne said. "But so is catching a killer, I imagine. You tell me: how do we start?"

"First, we have to narrow our suspect list," Brian said. "We don't have the manpower to investigate thousands of frustrated writers."

"What about the editors' log books?" Anne asked. "All editors are supposed to log manuscripts in when they arrive, then record the date they mail them back out."

"How's your log book?" Brian asked.

"Mine's four months behind, maybe five," Anne admitted. "But I haven't had an assistant for the past year. Logging is the assistant's job."

"Both victims were in the same position," Brian said. "One was five months behind, the other six."

"That means hundreds of manuscripts went in and out without anyone recording their passage," Anne said.

"That's the problem," Brian said. "But we can eliminate published writers and writers who haven't sent you anything lately. And if the killer got his manuscript back before he shot Jessica Brody, that book is probably already here in your office or will come in within the next week."

"That should narrow our suspects down to five or six hundred writers," Anne said.

"It's a start," Brian said. "Can you tell whether a manuscript is from someone who has been trying to get published for a long time or from a first-timer?"

"Yes, most first-timers give themselves away in the cover letter."

"Then we can eliminate them too. A first-timer wouldn't be frustrated enough to kill."

"You're right. Writers are the most hopeful people in the world.

How else could they face all that blank paper? Only when their second or third books get turned down by every publisher in town do they begin to get the message. It takes years of rejection to wear them out."

"If you'll start sorting through the manuscripts for the veteran losers, I'll read those books first for clues."

"Sounds like a lot of work on a long shot."

"If this case was a sure thing, I wouldn't be here."

Chapter 6

WHEN THEY RETURNED to Anne's office with coffee, the room was stuffy and too warm. "Can you turn down the heater?" Brian asked.

"It's only got two settings," Anne said, "too hot and not at all."

"Machines can be fixed, last I heard."

"First, you need a boss who wants to fix them. In publishing, they figure editors want to be here or we would go somewhere else and work half as hard for twice as much money."

Brian put the coffee cup down on his desk and took off his jacket, hanging it over the back of the chair.

"Here's something you don't see every day in a publishing house," Anne said.

"What?"

"Your gun." Anne pointed to the automatic in his shoulder holster. "If you wear it around the office, I'm going to have a hard time convincing people that you're my new assistant editor."

For Brian, wearing a gun around the office was something everyone did. He grinned and unstrapped the holster, looking for a place to conceal it. He sat down behind his desk and pulled the top drawer open.

The front of the drawer came off in his hands, and he toppled backwards out of the chair. He landed on his back holding the drawer by the handle.

When Anne stopped laughing, she said, "Sorry, I forgot about that. My last assistant took all the screws off that desk before he left."

"Why?"

"He wanted to leave his mark in publishing. What can I tell you? It's a screwy business."

As Brian started to get up, the office door opened and a guy who looked like the skipper of a yacht burst in. He was tall and aristocratic at 50, with luxurious silver hair that was made to be swept back by the wind and a patrician nose that gave him a good angle for looking down on everything. He wore a dark blue blazer with a sailing patch, gray wool slacks, and a red rep tie. He was darkly tanned.

He glanced at Brian, then strode over to Anne's desk, waving a bunch of pink message slips. "I hate messages, especially messages about you quitting." He threw the pink slips over his shoulder. "You're not quitting, are you?"

"This is Brandon Everall," Anne said, "the head of Everall Publishing." Brian stood up.

"You're the best mystery editor in the biz," Brandon said, ignoring Brian. "If you quit, I'll throw myself off the tallest library in New York City."

"Maybe we should talk about that raise now," Anne said.

"Of course, everyone has to leave sometime. I'll find a way to carry on." Brandon pointed at Brian. "Who's that and why was he lying around on my floor?"

Brian extended his hand. "Detective Brian Skiles, New York City Police Department."

Brandon folded his arms across his chest. "She's innocent. Why, even if Anne's guilty, she's still innocent. I don't care what she did, you can't take her away from me. Although, she could still edit from prison, I suppose."

"She's helping me with a murder investigation," Brian said.

"Not on my time, she's not. After hours, that's her business, although I would think knitting or model airplanes would be more suitable hobbies."

"Money," Anne said. "We're going to make you money."

"Why didn't you say so?" Brandon grabbed Brian's hand and pumped it. "Always glad to help the police. How much money?"

"Lots."

"My favorite kind."

"We're writing a book about catching the book killer," Anne said. "The one who murdered Jessica Brody over at Peters and Pryor."

"Yes, heard about that," Brandon said. "Terrible tragedy. But couldn't have happened to a better publishing house. Are you going to ghost the book out or write it yourself?"

"I write. He catches," Anne said. "We're planning to trap the killer here; so if anyone should ask, Brian's my new assistant editor."

"You're not putting him on salary?"

"No, but we don't want people to know he's a detective."

"Glad to do my part, and I shan't tell a soul. Mim's the word."

"Actually, mum's the word," Anne pointed out.

"Whatever," Brandon said. "I suppose you paid yourself a tremendous amount of money for the rights to the book?"

"No, I cheated myself on the royalties," Anne said.

"By God, I've always said you were a great editor."

"It's my theory that the killer . . ." Brian began.

"Good," Brandon interrupted. "Everyone should have a theory. Just don't tell me about it. I'm not a detail man. The important thing is there's no romance going on here, right?"

"Just murder," Brian said, not quite sure what the man meant.

"Because romance is more dangerous than murder. I couldn't handle it if you two fell in love."

Anne waved a hand in dismissal. "So far, we're not even sure we like each other."

"Only people who don't like each other can fall in love," Brandon said. "Don't you ever go to the movies?"

"You're getting out of line," Brian said.

"I was born out of line." Brandon reached over the desk and clasped Anne's hand. "You know you're the only woman for me. I'm mad for you. Crazy about you. Highly zonkers."

"That's why you've had affairs with every other woman editor on the staff." Anne pulled her hand away.

"I have my responsibilities as head of this great publishing house." Brandon took her hand again. "It would crush Claire if she was the only romance editor in town who wasn't having an affair with her high-powered, silver-haired boss. Then there's my fling with my science fiction editor, which puts a lot of pressure on me because every time we do it, it has to be out of this world. Of course, there are my writers, and you know I have to screw them. But, Anne, you're the only one I'm going to marry. As soon as I divorce Francoise."

"Do you people always talk about yourselves like you were a soap opera?" Brian asked.

"Doesn't everyone?"

"He doesn't understand, Brandon," Anne said. "He's from that world they call reality. He doesn't know how we live here in fantasy land."

"Swear you'll never leave me for him," Brandon said.

"Don't be silly," Anne said. "I'm not interested in either of you."

Brian got his shoulder holster from the drawer with the loose front. He strapped it on and headed for the door. "Don't let me interrupt you two," he said, "but I have a killer to catch. I'll be back after I report in to the captain."

"Make me money and hate each other," Brandon said. "That's all I ask."

Chapter 7

CAPTAIN HANK STARK didn't have his own secretary. He also didn't have a leather couch and two leather chairs in a waiting room outside his office. He didn't even have a waiting room.

Assistant Police Commissioner Farber Allen had the waiting room and the leather furniture and the secretary, and the secretary had long legs and wasn't particularly impressed by captains, especially short ones.

"You may go in now, Captain," the secretary said, giving him the kind of look a nurse gives a dental patient, knowing it's not her teeth that will be drilled.

Farber Allen came around his desk as Stark entered. "Just got the new espresso machine," Allen said. "You must have some." He shook Stark's hand, then went into the refreshment nook. Allen's office was twice as big as Stark's. His desk was twice as big. He was twice as big.

"I was at the ballet the other night," Allen said as he worked the handle of the espresso machine. "Don't suppose you go much to the ballet, Hank?"

"No, I go regularly," Stark said, wondering what he would put in his own office if he ever made assistant commissioner. A yogurt maker? "The ex-wife dragged me to it last year for my forty-seventh birthday when she found out that your wife drags you there. I plan to make the ballet a regular event. Go see one every forty-seven years."

Allen set a small espresso in front of Stark and put his own cup on top of a napkin on top of his desk blotter. He sat down in a chair that looked like a pilot's seat from *Star Wars.*

"At intermission I was speaking to Bill Peters," Allen said, "of Peters and Pryor Publishers. He asked me how the investigation into the murder of his mystery editor was going. Jessamyn Brooks, I believe."

"Jessica Brody."

"Whatever," Allen said. "So I had to give him some bull that I prefer to save for the press, where I can spread it around more."

"The significant lie at the proper moment," Stark said.

"Exactly. Anyway, Peters tells me that one of his writers has made him an interesting offer, the one who writes the series on Sri Laka, the Buddhist monk who lives on the Upper East Side and solves society murders in his spare time when he's not meditating."

"Never read that stuff," Stark said. "They always figure everything out, neat as a pin. Drives me nuts." He drank some of the espresso, thought it tasted bitter, then realized it was supposed to taste bitter. Good, though.

"Anyway," Allen said, "this writer offers to solve the murder of this editor if Peters will give him a hundred thousand reward."

"I'd like to see him try," Stark said. "A writer, what a joke."

"I wouldn't like to see him try," Allen said. "Because Peters then tells me that someone in his marketing department got hold of the idea and wants to open it up to the great unwashed, offer a million dollars to anyone who can solve the murder. Make it a contest."

"Would police be eligible?"

"For immediate dismissal," Allen said. "Peters says he hasn't gone for the idea yet, but he is thinking about it and the publicity it would bring his company."

"What a circus."

"That's why I bring it up. I do not want to turn this investigation into a three-ring circus. Or even a two-ring circus. Right now, we have the only ring in town, and I want it to stay that way. One way to keep everything under control would be to solve the murder. Have you solved the murder, Captain?"

"We think we're closing in on . . ."

"Save it for the press." Allen swallowed his espresso in one long gulp and put the cup to one side. He leaned forward, his chair raising him up so he seemed to loom across the desk. "The second way to stop the circus would be for you to defuse, confuse, distract, and mistrack all those other clowns getting in your way. Do you think you can do that, Captain?"

"Yes, sir."

"That's right. Naturally, I don't care how you do that. You might, for example, arrest a few people, which will discourage some of the amateurs and throw the rest onto the wrong track, which is where I like them. But I leave it entirely up to you."

"I understand."

"I thought you would. The last thing I want is for one of these amateurs to solve the murder. It looks bad at budget time when I have to ask for more money to give my captains a raise."

Chapter 8

BRIAN PARKED THE Duster in the main lot and walked down the row of graves past a dozen people, all silent and sad. Cemeteries were hushed like libraries, he thought, and God was the big librarian—checking them in and checking them out.

He knelt at his father's grave and thought: the Knicks, Dad, did you see them last night? That fast break in the fourth? They're going to catch Boston. I know they are.

And I'm going to catch this killer. But it's a bad case, you would see that, with too many suspects. Ten suspects are too many, five are. I've narrowed my list from several thousand to several hundred, only there are still no names on it. How can I handle a case like that, with Stark hostile and leading the primary investigation in another direction?

Reading the manuscripts is a waste of time; I know that. I don't expect to find clues that way. It's an excuse to stick around the bait so maybe I'll be there when the killer strikes again. This Anne

Baker, you'd go for her, Dad. This book she wants to write; it's the rope that holds the bait securely to the trap.

That boss of hers, a stupid man, frivolous, too rich, too amused by sucking all the cream out of life. It would be great if he were the killer, Brian thought. I'd like to see him try to do time.

All that office banter between Everall and Anne: I'm not a detail man. Hate each other; that's all I ask. Showing off their intimacy to an intruder. To them, I'm the civilian. Book banter.

We do it too. Cop banter. Jock banter. Trucker banter. Wherever you go, it's always us and them.

All their talk of romance, out of nowhere. I don't do romance, Brian thought. Once was enough. Love, marriage, it's unprofessional. The divorce courts and the bars are full of cops and cops' wives. No.

I've got my work, the paintings, and women like Janice last night. Or was it Janet? Women who came as strangers and left that way. It was Janice, pretty certain; give it a couple of days and it won't matter.

In a while, there will be another phone call from another woman. One who will go home in the morning. But Anne, I'd have to see again. At the office, full of her purpose and emotions. She has a right to that, but not to that and me.

Or worse, one morning I might not see her again. That's why I don't mix women and business. Lovers make lousy victims.

A man and a woman walked past Brian, on their way to another grave. He watched them moving, slowly, carefully, as if they would disturb someone.

They stood some ten graves away, heads bowed, silent. Brian looked at the stone on his father's grave: WILLIAM SKILES, MAY 14, 1935–SEPTEMBER 28, 1967. ALTERI SECULO.

It's strange, Brian thought, that this was all that was left of a man, that so much in life had gone into producing so little in death.

Serit arbores quae alteri seculo prosint. It was his mother's idea. "He plants trees to benefit another generation."

His mother was always reading when Brian was a boy. Anything old: the Greeks, Shakespeare, the poets Blake, Byron, Poe. When he was a teenager, he was glad his mother read all the time, so he didn't have to talk to her.

She remarried when the insurance money ran out. Billy away at college, Brian still in high school. But the widower she found had seen his own kids through their teenage years. He didn't want to go through that again with Brian, who got into fights at school.

His mother agreed to put Brian in a military academy, and the marriage went through. After school, he enlisted, was stationed in Europe. Learned a lot of things, few of them from the army. Came back to New York when he got out, and a police captain who had liked his father got him on the force.

His mother lived in Florida now with the man she had married. Definitely not *alteri seculo.* Brian saw her once a year, brought her a book.

Maybe I should go to Florida, Brian thought, retire my brain. Go to Jamaica or wherever else they have a beach. Get enough beer and a chair that faces the ocean and stare at the water until there isn't a thought in my head.

Other cops work the crime business out of their system that way. They come back and are better for it, feeling clear, clean. For a few days at least.

But you don't catch killers lying on the beach.

Brian closed his eyes. Now who thought that? he wondered.

Chapter 9

WHEN ANNE ARRIVED at Chez Adam, her two oldest friends in New York, Erin Ordo and Bissie Neece, were sitting at a table in the lounge evaluating two men at the bar. The men were young and looked both hip and rich.

"Let's get into the dining room quick" Bissie said. "One more drink and I'll pick up both of them."

The dining room was decorated in miniature trees, around each of which was a table. They were led to the miniature almond table, where Anne ordered a double stinger to catch up.

"I was telling Erin about this audition I went to," Bissie said as they eyed the other people in the room. "It was for an Off, and I'd heard the director had a thing for blondes. So I borrowed a blonde wig from Felissa to do the audition. Did it good too. Then he tells me, close but he's really looking for a brunette. So I whip off the wig and say, here I am. And he shakes his head and says, 'No, I really see you as a blonde. The brunette isn't working for me.' "

"Directors," Erin said.

"Men," Anne said.

The waiter set their drinks down on top of cocktail napkins that said *Chez Adam, the first name in fine dining.*

"My name is Perkins," the waiter said, "and I'll be your guide for the meal."

"What's to eat?" Erin asked.

"Two specials tonight," Perkins said. "The Scallop Linguini Maria. Maria was Chef Ramone's first lover of the new year. Maria, who left Chef for the baker at the Cafe Fritz. It's a lovely dish, exuberantly creamy with a tragic touch of tarragon to remind us all of the romance and sorrow that make such exquisite dining possible."

"Anything in a burger?" Bissie asked. "I'm in a burger mood."

"The Hamburger Jim," Perkins said. "Jim blew into town a few weeks ago, made everyone examine the dark side of their souls, and then he was gone. Chef has captured Jim in bleu cheese with a fleck of jalapeño to hint at something deeper."

"That's me tonight," Bissie said. "The Hamburger Jim."

"I'm the Bisque Andy," Erin said, "and the Sid Salad."

"And who might you be tonight?" Perkins asked Anne.

"Do you have anything named for someone daring and wildly rich?"

"The Lamb Steak Wilette," Perkins said, "for the woman who

tried to swim the Panama Canal. Chef Ramone has honored her with garlic puree and hazelnut creme."

When Anne had ordered a bottle of white zinfandel and Perkins had left, Erin asked, "Why do you feel so daring tonight, Annie?"

"I'll tell you later," Anne said. "I want to hear the latest chapter of The Story of John. What have you done about him?"

"John the abstract expressionist or John the art supply salesman?" Erin asked.

"John who's been getting you all that marble," Anne said.

"Beautiful slabs," Erin said. "I see bodies in it, faces, all things round and libidinous. It's like I'm not the sculptor. I'm the person chosen to release the shapes that nature locked in the marble."

"Artists," Bissie said. "What did you do with John?"

"I sent him back to his wife and kids."

"I thought you did that last month," Anne said.

"I've thrown him out half a dozen times," Erin said. "But he's so sweet, I always let him come back. It's too much trouble to get him to fight so we can break up properly."

"What can you expect from a married man?" Bissie asked.

"It's true," Erin said. "They're so sick of fighting with their wives, they never give you any trouble."

"Then why get rid of him?" Anne asked.

Erin waited while Perkins uncorked the wine. He poured a taste into each of their glasses. "Chef is pleased with your orders tonight," he said. "He senses that you are establishing a deeper friendship that in the long run will be more satisfying than any short-term diets." The three women nodded over their wine, and he poured their glasses full.

The women toasted. "To Bryn," Erin said.

"To Mawr," Bissie said.

"What for?" Anne said.

They drank. "So tell," Bissie said.

"His wife kept bugging me," Erin said. "At first, she'd call and ask me to get John to pick up some milk for the kids on his way home. Or she'd want me to remind him to transfer money into their joint checking account so she could pay the bills."

"She sounds good," Anne said.

"Right, gave me a first class case of the guilts," Erin said. "Then we started having these long chats on the phone about John's low self-esteem and his sense of insecurity. She was so nice I couldn't stand it. I began to see why he cheated on her. I felt like cheating on her myself. That's when I realized I had to get rid of him. Or invite them both to move into my loft. Bring the kids. What the hell."

Perkins brought their food. "I'd love to stay longer, but we have a couple in from Connecticut who need my help."

"What are you going to do next?" Bissie asked. "Go back to John the abstract expressionist?"

"First, no more Johns in my life," Erin said. "What I really want is a man as good as a Braun electrical appliance."

"Do tell," Anne said. "Exactly what is your favorite electrical appliance?"

"No, I mean if you have a blender and it breaks down, you don't try to fix it. It's simpler to go out and get another one. You don't have to relate to your blender."

"Disposable men with replaceable parts," Bissie said, "that may work for you. But I need to experience the entire range of human emotions so when I'm on the stage I look like I'm having them. For all those dramatic emotions like pain and sorrow, you need a real man to mess up your life. Thank God there are so many of them around. I can be miserable whenever I have to."

"Who are you miserable with now?" Erin asked.

"I met this guy who programs lighting systems for concerts," Bissie said. "We've been on again, off again, that kind of affair. Then I'm at his place one night and wake up and hear him in the other room. I call him to come back to bed, and he says, 'Not now, I'm networking.' "

Anne split the last of the wine just as Perkins appeared with a second bottle. "My intuition told me this was called for," he said. "Don't crush me by sending it back."

"Pour," Anne said. Then after he had gone away again, "Tell."

"Networking," Bissie said. "Then I went in and found him playing with his computer. All humped over and touching it like he had never touched me. I felt like I had invaded the last bastion of male privacy. If men could program a computer for romance, they'd never need women again."

"How perfect for Annie," Erin said.

"Don't tell me you're still on strike," Bissie said.

"I'm not on strike," Anne said. "I chose to be celibate, and it's worked for me."

"How long has it been?" Erin asked. "Six months, ten days, four hours and fifty-two minutes?"

"Old joke," Anne said. "I don't keep count. But I have gotten two raises during that time, and I can finish the *New York Times* Sunday puzzle."

"I still don't get the point," Bissie said.

"I wanted something different in my life," Anne said. "I used to meet a guy, and maybe I'd think I was in love with him, or he'd think he was in love with me; neither of us knowing what we were supposed to do about it. Not marriage. Maybe a relationship, a brief moment. Confusion was the only thing I was sure about. I didn't want to be that confused. Lovers circle each other. I needed to go straight forward. Now that I'm celibate, I know I'm not in love."

"Are you any less confused?" Erin asked.

"No, but I have less to be confused about."

"Then what are you being so daring about?"

"I *have* met a guy," Anne said. "Only he's a cop."

"You're kidding," Bissie said. "What did you get busted for?"

"Nothing."

"Just like a cop to bust you for nothing," Bissie said. "Sue him for false arrest."

"He wants me to help him solve a case. Someone's been killing book editors. Brian thinks I'm the next target. We're setting a trap for the killer."

"What are you, the bait?" Erin asked.

"I'm his partner," Anne said.

"Romance, intrigue, murder," Bissie said. "I love it."

"I could never get interested in a man who wears a gun," Anne said. "Guns are so symbolic. I can't handle heavy symbolic relationships."

As they finished the second bottle of wine, Bissie said, "Look at us. We've either got the wrong man or someone else's or none at all. They promised us we would be wildly happy and rich and look like a magazine ad. I don't mind being tough and crazy, but things are supposed to work out for people like us."

"If I wasn't so depressed all the time, I'd kill myself," Erin said.

"You two remember the vow we took at Bryn Mawr," Anne said. "No matter what happened to us, we would never give in. We would always be different."

"Yes."

"Well, girls, looks like we made it," Anne said.

Chapter 10

BRIAN FOUND AL VISO down at Brown's, a block from the precinct house, eating a Salisbury steak with mushroom gravy that was the same color as the coffee he was drinking.

Brian sat down and Al looked across the table at him, chewing steadily. "This our ten year reunion?" he asked.

"I've been busy," Brian said.

Corly came over and set a coffee in front of Brian. "Eat?" she asked. Brian shook his head, and she went away.

"What are you working on?" Brian asked.

"Too much." Al pushed his plate away. "These people in the book biz, they move around all the time, from one publisher to the next, sometimes back again. So far, we've talked to fifty-four of them who worked with both editors—Amy Johnson, the first one, and Jessica Brody, the second one—at five different publishers over the past six years. Most of these people probably had keys to both offices. Publishers don't change locks when someone leaves because they'd have to employ permanent locksmiths and besides they figure there's nothing much to steal."

"If they move around so much, the two vics ever cross?"

"Yes, five years ago both Brody and Johnson worked at a place called Vargas House for a few months."

"Anything from that?"

"Not yet." Al signaled for Corly to take his plate away. She refilled both cups with coffee that looked like gravy. "Then there are the people who worked with only one of the editors but knew the other one from conferences, trade associations, parties. We haven't even started on them. We've got us a world of connections here, and the more we look the more we find."

"What's it look like outside the business?"

"Brody was married, but had four affairs in the past two years, as far as we've gotten, all with actors, guys in soaps produced here in Manhattan. That seems to have been her specialty, soap guys."

"And Johnson was married with no known affairs, last time I checked," Brian said.

"Still nothing, but we have found out what she did in her free time. Analysis. She had more shrinks than the other one had lovers, six in the past two years."

Brian looked into his coffee cup and wondered how the first person in history had ever been convinced to drink something that looked like mud and often tasted that way too. "Any witnesses turn up?"

"We finally got to the sandwich delivery boy," Al said.

"This the Brody killing?"

"Yeah, the other one was on a diet. The boy says he went up, she met him at the door, he gave her the pastrami and left. We checked out his other deliveries that night, and it looks like he stayed right on schedule."

"What about Johnson's husband, the caterer? Anything new from him?"

"Herb Johnson," Al said. "His mother-in-law says they fought a lot. The usual things, but not money. They both made enough. We haven't established any relationship between Herb and the second, Jessica Brody. What have you been working on?"

"I'm still looking into the writer angle," Brian said.

"Frustrated writer kills the editors who reject his books?"

"It establishes an instant connection between the victims and an instant motive."

"Also instant headaches," Al said. "Since the captain doesn't buy it, how are you going to handle such a big investigation yourself?"

Brian shrugged. "Maybe I'll get Stark to change his mind."

"Now there's an idea whose time has yet to come." Al signaled Corly for the check. "He doesn't mind if you stay away from him, why should you?"

"I want some back-up."

"Yeah? You're going to get your back up against a wall. You're a good detective, Brian. If you're going to be a jerk, why couldn't you be a bad detective so I wouldn't mind losing you?"

Chapter 11

BRIAN SAW THE TV news vans parked in front of the precinct house, so he wasn't surprised to find Captain Stark holding a press conference in the duty room. Stark stood on the platform duty sergeants used for tour briefings, which de-emphasized his lack of height.

Brian leaned against the wall and watched the captain work the cameras. "We know the killer was a friend of the victim," Stark said, "or someone she worked with."

"How do you know that?" one of the reporters asked.

"The killer didn't break into the office," Stark said. "He used a key or the editor let him in. At that time of night, working alone, she wouldn't have let in a stranger."

"What's the connection between this murder and the death of the mystery editor from Joss House?" a second reporter asked.

"Both editors were killed with the same gun." Stark consulted his notebook. "A Webley-Fosbery thirty-eight automatic eight shot. They don't make them any more."

Anne was working on the book in her apartment, sitting at the old walnut desk with the even older Royal typewriter, roughing out the chapter that would deal with how she and Brian had joined forces to trap the book killer.

The walls of her writing room were lined with bookcases and framed prints. The couch and stuffed chairs and oak table had come from her grandmother, the writing desk and typewriter from her great-uncle, who had been a doctor, an attorney, and a poet.

The only modern furniture in the room was a chrome shelf that held three TV sets. When Anne wrote, which wasn't often any more, she turned on all three sets to produce a kind of visual white noise.

Out of that visual white noise, Anne picked up Captain Stark's press conference running live on two channels. She stopped typing to watch.

"Were the two women editors involved in a love triangle?" a reporter asked.

"We're looking into that possibility," Stark said.

"Love triangle?" Anne said aloud, although she was alone in the room. "With Jessica, it would have been a love octagon."

"There's a rumor going around that the killer left a message for the police," another reporter said. "Any comment?"

"No, but I have a message for the killer," Stark said. "We're going to get you, and soon."

"No arrests, please," Anne said. "I'm only on chapter two."

Captain Stark waited until the reporters had left the duty room before he climbed off the platform and returned to his office. Brian followed him in.

"Got a minute?"

"Depends," Stark said. "You want to tell me how well I handle the press, I got the time. You got another crazy theory, I'm all out of time. And so are you."

"I'm setting a trap for the killer," Brian said.

"Are you? And who is the killer?"

"Like I said, a writer who can't stand rejection," Brian said. "I can trap him, but I need some back up."

"You think I've got the manpower to investigate twenty thousand suspects?"

"Not that many."

"You've got it all wrong," Stark said. "We have a simple double murder here. That's all. We find the person who knew both women and had motive and opportunity, and we'll solve the case. I have enough crazies in this city. I don't have to go looking for a lunatic writer who kills editors because they won't publish his book."

"We're not back on the street busting in doors," Brian said. "We've got to find the right door, the one the killer's behind."

"You make me laugh, Skiles. You've got twice the brains of a guy like me and half the smarts. There's more to police work than solving the crime."

"No, that's all there is."

"You have to take a broader view of the whole crime-society gestalt," Stark said. "There's a lot of madness in the world and it scares people. You try to deal with the madness; that's why you never get anywhere. I deal with the fear; that's why they give me whatever I want."

"That's sick."

"That's life. Wise up."

Brian started out of the office, then turned back. "How many more editors have to be killed before you'll admit you might be wrong?"

"One more." Stark stood up behind his desk, his chiseled face suddenly red. "That's how many. One more editor gets gunned down, and I'll think we might have a problem on our hands. But that won't matter to you because you're off the case."

"Partners don't do that to each other."

"We haven't been partners in years. Forget about it. I have."

All three TV stations had commercials on at the same moment, which provided the perfect white visuals for Anne as she wrote a chapter about herself—a subject which had to be fascinating for the book to succeed.

The doorbell rang. Anne ignored it, absorbed in ways to make an editor's life sound more glamorous. She gave up on the third ring, lacking the endurance to shut out the world entirely.

When she opened the door, Brandon Everall lurched at her. She blocked the doorway, and he stumbled backwards, swinging a bottle of champagne in one hand. "I've decided it's time I made love to you," he said.

"You'd better get your watch fixed," Anne said.

"Aren't you going to let me in?" Brandon took a step back, ready to charge.

"This is my sanctuary," Anne said. She braced herself against the doorframe. "The only person I entertain here is myself."

Brandon tried to squeeze past her, but she pushed him back. He ran a hand through his spray of white hair. "You won't let me in because you have him in there."

"Who?"

"That cop. That illiterary. That killer's Boswell."

"Don't be absurd," Anne said. "I wouldn't have him in here even more than I wouldn't have you. I'm doing something you will like even more than making love to me."

"Do tell."

"I'm working on the book that will buy your second yacht or your third car or your fourth estate. I want to have it finished as soon as we catch the killer so we can break the case and the best-seller list at the same time. Think of the publicity. Think of the sales."

Brandon leaned in close. "You have no idea how much money turns me on." She ducked his kiss, and he planted it on the wall. He wiped his mouth on his sleeve, then dusted his arm. "What turns me off is you making love with that cop, who couldn't write his way out of a traffic ticket. I'm far too rich to be rejected."

"I haven't touched him." Anne put both hands on Brandon's shoulders and turned him around. "But if you don't leave me alone, I will."

Chapter 12

IN THE LOBBY of the editorial offices, the receptionist Melanie Armatraz was beginning a new science fiction novel when the door opened and a short, intense man came in carrying a briefcase. "I'm here to see your mystery editor," he said.

"Do you have an appointment?" Melanie hoped he did because this was the kind of man who would annoy Anne Baker.

"I do." The man pulled out a ten dollar bill. "Mr. Hamilton."

Melanie looked at the appointment book on her desk. "I have nothing for a Mr. Hamilton," she said. "But I do have an appointment for Mr. . . . um . . . Jackson."

He grimaced but gave her a twenty, which she put in her pocket. "First door on the left," she said.

When the office door opened and the short, intense man entered, Anne knew what he was right away. The man stopped inside the door and opened his briefcase. Brian slipped off the front of the desk drawer with no screws and put his hand on the gun inside the drawer.

"Sorry," Anne said, "no writers. I never see writers."

"I'm glad to hear that," the man said, pulling a manuscript from the briefcase, "because I wouldn't want to make a million dollars for an editor who did. I'm Dr. Don Dooley, your next best-selling author."

Brian took his hand off the gun and looked the man over. Dr.

Dooley was in his late forties, with thinning black hair and seagreen eyes. He had the thin, ropey body of a runner, covered with an expensive gray suit.

"Your manuscript can stay," Anne told him, "but you'll have to leave."

"And what a manuscript!" Dr. Dooley said. "You want murders? I've got a higher murder-per-chapter ratio than Mickey Spillane."

"Stop," Anne said, looking both grim and bored. She had been through this before too many times.

"And mystery?" Dr. Dooley said. "Why some of my solutions are so tricky, I can't even figure them out myself."

"Enough," Anne said. "Get out." She looked over at Brian.

As Brian circled around his desk, Dr. Dooley backed away, holding his manuscript in front of him like a matador's cape, moving lightly on the balls of his feet like a boxer.

"You're probably asking yourself, does my book have sex?" Dr. Dooley said as he danced away from Brian.

"No," Anne said. "I'm not."

"It has great sex," Dr. Dooley said. "And lousy sex." Brian lunged for him, but he circled away.

"Out," Anne ordered.

"Safe sex." Dooley's words came out in short bursts as he began to get winded from dodging and talking at the same time. "And dangerous sex."

"Out, out, out."

"But best yet, I'm a licensed psychiatrist." Dooley stopped flat-footed at this last pronouncement, and Brian grabbed him. "I understand what motivates people to buy books."

Brian started moving Dooley toward the door. Dooley didn't resist. He also didn't stop talking. "And for a limited time only, if you buy my book, I'll cure the neurosis of your choice."

Brian stopped suddenly and Dooley yanked his arm free, which swung the manuscript into Brian's face, knocking him down. Dooley looked at Brian in shock. "Oh, no, now I've done it. I've hit an editor."

"Don't worry," Anne said. "He's only an assistant editor."

Dooley helped Brian to his feet. "I think Dr. Dooley may qualify for our unknown writer's program," Brian said.

"You do?" Anne asked, wondering what Brian was up to and where he had found the nerve to take charge in her office.

"He may be exactly the person we're looking for."

"I see," Anne said because she knew it was a good thing to say when you didn't see.

Brian turned toward Dooley. "Have you been trying to get your books published for a long time?"

"Too long," Dr. Dooley said. "Although I'm okay about that."

"And have you been rejected by so many editors that you've grown frustrated with the system?" Brian asked.

"Yes, but I can deal with that."

Anne saw what Brian was up to, although she hoped Dooley didn't. "You do sound like the kind of person our new program has been designed for," she said.

"Yes, I thrive on rejection," Dooley said. "One must thrive on rejection if one lives in New York."

"Here at Everall Publishing we realize that all the great writers were at first rejected by dozens of publishers," Anne said. "James Joyce, Sinclair Lewis, Dr. Seuss."

"That's why we want to find the best unknown rejected writers and publish them," Brian said.

"This is wonderful," Dooley said, "because I've been rejected by the best. Here, I have their rejection slips to prove it." He opened his briefcase and took out a bulging folder.

"You carry them around with you?" Brian asked.

"Only to prove it doesn't bother me," Dooley said.

"This sounds very promising," Brian said.

"Tell us a little about your book, Dr. Dooley," Anne said.

"It's called *The Inner Murders,*" Dooley said. "It's about a psychiatrist who solves a series of murders in which all the victims die psychologically."

"That sounds like an interesting new twist," Anne said.

"I specialize in twists," Dooley said. "As a licensed psychiatrist,

I've learned that everyone has murderous urges. That's why there's so much killing. But murder can be a healthy impulse as long as it's fictional. It's only when murder becomes real that it indicates the killer may have a personality problem."

"Let us read your manuscript, Dr. Dooley," Brian said. "We'll get back to you right away."

Dooley set his manuscript on Anne's desk. "If you have any problems, I can fix them. Whatever it is—the title, the story, the words—don't worry, I can change it."

"You'll hear from us soon," Anne said.

Dr. Dooley slowly opened the door and reluctantly left. Anne reached for the manuscript. "Don't touch it," Brian said. He used a ruler to push the manuscript into a large envelope.

"What are you doing?" Anne asked.

"I need his fingerprints to find out if he has a police record," Brian said. "Do writers often bring their books into the office in person like Dr. Dooley?"

Anne tilted her head to the side and looked at Brian. This ordinary appearance of his, she thought, it was all a fraud. Behind his lack of assertiveness, there was a very persistent character.

"No," she said. "Most writers have the modesty to mail them. The ones who come here thinking they can talk me into buying their books are almost always the very worst writers. What's the point?"

"I've been trying to figure out how the killer identifies his victims," Brian said.

Anne shrugged. "He kills whichever editor rejects his book. That's simple enough. Reject a book, bang you're dead."

"Yes, but if the killer is an unknown writer, then you'd be as unknown to him as he is to you."

"So what? Killers need a formal introduction to their victims?"

"How did he know what Amy Johnson looked like if he sat at home and waited for the post office to deliver his book? How would he know which office was Jessica Brody's? He'd have to see his intended victims at work first."

"Which he could do if he is one of the writers who bring in their books," Anne said.

"Which only the most aggressive writers have the nerve to do," Brian said. "And murder is certainly an aggressive act. People who have time to wait for a mailman aren't frustrated enough to kill. Dr. Dooley, on the other hand, is desperate enough to try anything."

"There's something I want you to do for me," Anne said.

"What?"

"Arrest Dr. Dooley."

"But there will be other writers who try to get back here," Brian said. "I can't arrest them all."

"Why not?"

"It wouldn't solve our problem," Brian said. "It would only let the killer know we were on to him and he would go on to another publishing house and find another victim."

"That would solve my problem," Anne said, "which is staying alive."

"But it wouldn't get you a best-selling book."

"It's scary talking to a killer like he was a normal person."

"You get used to it after a while."

"That's easy for you to say," Anne said. "He's not out to kill you."

"I'm going to open a file on Dr. Dooley," Brian said. "Meanwhile, let's take a look at the other writers who bring their books into the office."

"The front desk manages to stop most of them."

"From now on, let them come back."

Anne went over to the coat rack, put on her long gray cloth coat and her black gloves. "Let's go to lunch. You can make sure no one tries to poison my mushroom flambé."

Brian put on his shoulder holster and his coat and followed Anne into the lobby to the receptionist's desk. "Brian, this is Ms. Armatraz, keeper of the gate and gossip command central. Melanie, this is Mr. Skiles, my new assistant editor."

"I knew when you told me you were a cop yesterday that you weren't a cop," Melanie said.

"How could you tell?" Brian asked.

"You didn't look shot enough." Melanie Armatraz was a sleepy-eyed redhead in her early twenties with hair that shone like a fire reflected in gold.

"It was just a gag," Brian said. "I bet Anne that I could get back to see her without having an appointment. You must have writers try that all the time."

"I try to stop them," Melanie said. "But writers are tricky." She put her hand in her pocket and rubbed Dr. Dooley's twenty dollars.

"We've solved that problem for you," Anne said. "Now that I have Brian to assist me, I've decided to see them all. Maybe I'll discover a great writer that way."

Melanie looked over at Anne, wondering why this particular editor always went out of her way to cause trouble. "You want me to let them go back there?"

"Yes."

"Boy, I don't know about this writing business," Melanie said, tossing her red hair so Brian could get the full effect.

"It's pretty tough, isn't it?" Brian asked as Anne pulled him toward the door.

"Tough?" Melanie said. "It's murder."

Chapter 13

THE WIND WHIPPED snow into their faces as they left the building. Brian looked up at the sky, while Anne checked out the sidewalk. The sky was light, and the snow wasn't sticking.

Anne turned up the collar of her coat and wrapped a brown woolen scarf around it. Brian hunkered down into his jacket and wondered why, after all these years in New York, he still didn't dress for the weather.

They headed toward Fifth Avenue. Across the street, Dr. Don Dooley stood in a doorway and aimed a Nikon at them. He focused the zoom lens and snapped off a dozen shots before they turned the corner.

Anne pulled the scarf away from her mouth and leaned close to Brian as they walked. "So are you married, divorced, or gay?"

"Why do you ask? I'm not a suspect here."

"It's for the book," Anne said. "We need something to fill in the pages between the violence and the sex."

"How do you know there's going to be sex?" Brian asked.

"There always is." Anne brushed snow out of her eyes. "I'd guess divorced and glad of it."

"I got married in my first year on the force," Brian said. "Rookie mistake. What about you?"

"Not me. I work twelve hours a day. Then I go home and think about books. Marriage is for people who don't have anything else to do."

"Murder is better than marriage," Brian said, thinking about Cathy. "In murder you don't have any problem figuring out who the victim is."

"This is it." Anne opened the door of the Cookbook Cafe. Inside, the walls were papered with the covers of hundreds of cookbooks. "Everything on the menu is from a cookbook published by one of the New York houses."

"Kind of like eating your own, isn't it?" Brian asked.

Anne took off her coat and hung it up. "That's why so many people from the business come here." They waited for the busy maître d'.

"Something's been bothering me," Brian said. "If you can write books, why do you work as an editor?"

"Because I'm smart," Anne said. "When I got out of college, I moved to the Village determined to become the great American writer. Then I did what most writers do—got a job waiting tables in a cheap bar. I wrote during the day, first a novel, then another one. I sent them off to every publishing house in town, looking for someone who could recognize greatness. But they always got sent back by editors with the sensitivity of slugs. Finally, I decided it was better to reject people then get rejected. I had gone to Bryn Mawr, which meant I qualified for an entry-level job at a publishing house. From there, I worked my way up, which wasn't that hard because a lot of people who were up ahead of me kept bailing out."

The maître d' led them through the crowded dining room. Brian watched as various people gave Anne the slightest nod of recognition and she gave them the slightest nod back.

As soon as they were seated, a waiter came over. "I'll have the usual," Anne said. "Bring him something red and still growling."

"Pastrami, rye, Russian, slaw," Brian said.

"Would you prefer the *Joy of Cooking* recipe or the *I Remember Mama's Cooking* version?" the waiter asked.

"Make it *Joy,*" Brian said.

A woman slipped into the chair next to Anne. She was in her forties and wore a blue bow around her neck. She smiled at Brian.

"And who do you have here, Anne?" the woman asked, "or wherever it is you have him."

"My new assistant editor Brian Skiles," Anne said. "Glenda here pretends to edit books for a company that pretends to be a publishing house."

Glenda reached across the table and put her hand over Brian's. "You must come to work for me when you get tired of our little Annie. I have all her old assistants."

Another woman slipped into the chair across from Glenda. She was in her fifties and wore a pink bow around her neck. "Did you hear about poor Jessica Brody? They say her husband shot her because she was having an affair with that Welsh poet."

"Don't be silly," Glenda said. "Her husband shot her because she found out that *he* was having an affair with that Welsh poet."

The waiter set a martini in front of Anne and a platter in front of Brian. The two women looked at the food on his plate and left.

"There's a theory going around that you can put on weight simply by looking at food," Anne said. "You really should drink something. This is lunch."

"I don't drink while I'm working." He picked up his sandwich and began to eat quickly. Cops eat quickly because they don't like to tie up their hands.

"Really?" Anne said. "In my job, I have to."

"All those manuscripts I've been reading," Brian said, "they're terrible."

"Yes, I know."

"But if they're so bad, why do people send them in? And if people are going to send them in, why don't they write them better?"

"Because most people who think they can write a good mystery can't," Anne explained.

Brian finished half his sandwich. "Is it that tough to do?"

"Yes and no," Anne said, "like anything else. A good mystery only has to do one thing: keep readers interested from the first page through the last. The problem with most books is the story runs out long before the last page."

As Brian finished his pastrami, a man in his sixties sat down. He wore a blue bow tie with pink polka dots. "Did you hear about Jessica?" he asked. "They say her publisher killed her because she hadn't had a best-seller in ten months."

The waiter put the check down and said, "That's what everyone was saying yesterday. Today they say that *she* killed herself because she hadn't had a best-seller in ten months."

The man glanced at the check and, by instinct, headed toward the men's room. Brian reached for it, but Anne put her hand over his. "Assistant editors don't pay for lunch," she said.

"I hope I'm not interrupting anything."

As Brian's mouth dropped open, Anne turned and saw a startlingly beautiful blonde in a fur coat standing behind her. She looked like a dancer or an Olympic swimmer, but not at all like an editor.

"Hello, Brian," she said.

"Hello, Cathy."

"Perhaps I'm interrupting something," Anne said.

"No, we were interrupted a long time ago," Cathy said.

"Anne, this is my wife, Cathy McDougald."

"You mean your ex-wife," Anne said.

"Didn't I say that? My ex-wife. We're divorced."

"Why don't you sit down, Cathy," Anne said, "while Brian searches for his brains."

Cathy took off the fur coat and tossed it across one chair. She sat in the other. She wore a black leotard and a blue denim skirt over black tights. Her long, bare arms were tan and muscular. "I have to get back to teach an aerobics class for body-builders." She smiled at Anne. "I'm an instructor at the East Side Fitness Emporium. Brian and I met at the club, you know."

"No doubt you were sweating at the time," Anne said.

"That was a long time ago," Brian said.

"Seven years," Cathy said. "We were married a year after we met, but those times were so much more romantic than they are now. Don't you agree?"

"And what a coincidence, your showing up at this particular restaurant and here we are too," Anne said.

"I followed you here," Cathy said. "Now don't give me that funny look, Brian. You can't expect a person to be married to a cop for three years and not pick up a few tricks of the trade."

"How long have you been following me?" Brian asked.

"Don't get paranoid, Brian," Cathy said. "I happened to have a meeting at Everall Publishing. As I was leaving, I saw you. So I decided to say hi. It's been a long time."

"Who were you meeting with at Everall?" Anne asked.

"That charming publisher of yours, Brandon," Cathy said. "To discuss my new book. I think he's going to make me a very interesting offer."

"I'm sure he is," Anne said. "But what about your book?"

"It's the total fitness book for the total woman," Cathy said. "Exercise, sexercise, and relaxercise. Now that I've taken charge of my body, I'm ready to take charge of everyone else's. You ought to come down to the club, Anne. I'd put you through a workout that would really do you a lot of good."

"Not me," Anne said. "God made us with built-in obsolescence, and you can't fool the manufacturer. But you two probably want to talk after all these years. I've got to get back to work anyway."

"Don't run off on my account," Cathy said.

"Anne, I'll go back with you," Brian said. "Just give me a minute with Cathy."

"Fine, I'll wait in the bar."

"She's sweet," Cathy said when Anne had left.

"Not so you'd notice," Brian said. "How about you?"

"You used to think I was sweet. But let's not dwell on the past. How have you been? Still after the bad guys of the world?"

"That's what I do," Brian said. "I haven't changed."

"I have," Cathy said. "I'm much more complete than I used to be. I'm experiencing the total me."

Brian held up his hand like he was stopping traffic. "Cathy, why did you come here?"

"I wanted to see you again, make sure you were okay. It's been a long time."

"You've had four years to see if I was okay. Why now?"

"I'm seeing someone." She folded her arms across her chest and looked away.

He looked at the muscles in her arms. "You never needed to tell me before when you were seeing someone."

"This is different. It's someone you know."

"Who?"

"It's Hank Stark."

Brian thought of several things to say but managed to keep himself from saying any of them. He stood up. "I've got to get back to work," he said. Cathy nodded and looked down.

Brian was silent and gloomy as he and Anne walked back to the office. "Everything okay?" she asked.

"You've never been married, right?"

"No."

"Because if you had, you wouldn't ask questions like that," Brian said. "Everything is never okay."

Anne wrapped the scarf higher around her throat. The snow had stopped, but the wind hadn't. "She must have been very bouncy to be married to."

"Do me a favor and let's not talk about her."

"Fine with me. I've gone for years not talking about your ex-wife. I guess I can get along without it now."

They walked in silence for a block. Then Brian said, "When you go to lunch, don't you ever eat lunch?"

"In the book business, if you're not out there at lunch gossiping about them, they'll be out there gossiping about you," Anne said.

They reached the Everall building and rode the elevator up to the twentieth floor. "No one in your business seems very upset that two editors have been murdered in the past two months," Brian said.

Anne shrugged. "Editors come and go. Murder, suicide, burn out. They quit and get fired so fast we should use generic business cards. You know what we call a rookie in the book biz?"

"What?"

"A veteran."

Chapter 14

THE TWO PSYCHIATRISTS were stopped as they crossed the lobby by a woman who asked Dr. Paul Loring for his autograph. She held out Loring's latest best-seller and a pen.

Dr. Don Dooley waited patiently since no one had asked him to sign anything. And he didn't have a book to sign anyway.

The pen had run out of ink. The woman smiled sheepishly. Insecure, Dooley thought.

"No problem," Loring said. "I always carry two pens with me. One never knows." He slipped a pen from his pocket, flourished a scrawl inside the book, and smiled at the woman.

"Your books have really helped me," she said.

Brown nose, Dooley thought.

"That's why I write them," Loring said.

And you were a twerp in school, Dooley thought.

The woman smiled and backed away, clutching her book to her chest as if its value had somehow increased by having the author sign it.

"Sign a book, sell two," Loring said to Dooley as they continued across the lobby and into the hotel bar. "That's my motto."

"Everyone should have a motto," Dooley said as they sat at a corner table and ordered stingers.

"So how are you, Don?" Loring asked, looking Dooley over as if he were about to make an analysis of the situation. "Put on a few since I was in town last."

"No, actually I'm the same," Dooley said. "I've been working out. Muscles just make you look bigger."

"TV makes you look bigger too," Loring said. "You saw me on Carson, of course? A great guy. Says, 'Paul, drop by when you're out in Hollywood.' Get this: he wants me to analyze the woman next time he thinks of getting married. Let him know if it's a good idea, psychodynamically speaking."

"I hear Hollywood is very psychodynamic these days," Dooley said.

"Great opportunities," Loring said. "Of course, you've got to have the credentials: a best-seller, a radio talk show, something. All my patients are important people now."

"There are no little people," Dooley said. "Only little problems."

"Yes, but important people take up so much of one's time. There simply aren't enough hours in the day to help out the ordinary guy. Autographs, sure. Analysis, sorry, pal, try someone else."

"Why do you think people want autographs, anyway?" Dooley asked, signalling the waiter for another round.

"Actually, they see famous people like me and they'd like to sleep with us," Loring said. "But they're too embarrassed to ask for that, so they ask for our autographs instead. I'm thinking of writing a book about it."

"You've written a book about everything else."

"Three best-sellers in a row," Loring said.

"You'd think with all the help you've given people, they wouldn't need much more help," Dooley said.

"That's life. Also books," Loring said. "I ever tell you how I got going in this racket?"

"You mean, the patient with the cousin who worked for Doubleday?"

"No, the cousin was only the beginning," Loring said. "When you're starting out, you think it's hard to write a book. Then you realize that writing is easy compared to getting published. Even if you're good enough to get published, what do you really have? A pile of books. Doesn't mean anyone is going to buy them. Most cases, they won't. So if you're smart, you take matters into your own hands and do something about it."

"What?" Dooley asked. "What, exactly, can you do about anything?" He emptied his glass and held up the empty for the waiter to see.

"First, it helps to have a large family," Loring said. "Even better if they're strategically located in major cities across the country. Take my family. We're big and we stick together. Together, we bought up 10,000 copies of my first book. Cost me $170,000, but I sold them off again to used bookstores for $60,000."

"Which book was this?" Dooley interrupted.

"*It's Okay to Be Thin: Getting Rid of Psychological Fat.*"

"Didn't read it."

"Nobody did at first. That's why I mortgaged the house and bought them myself," Loring explained. "I'm down a hundred and twenty thou, but I look upon that as an investment because selling 10,000 copies convinced my publisher that he had a potential best-seller on his hands. So he starts printing more, gives me the advertising, puts me on the talk shows, the lecture circuit. And I do okay. I got my one-liners down. Sold 100,000 copies, for which I make $160,000, which puts me $80,000 ahead of the game. Plus, I get $100,000 advance on my next book. Yeah, literature, ain't it great?"

Fixated on numbers, Dooley thought. And it's well known that the larger the number fixation, the smaller the penis. It was pitiful, really, that Loring, who had been a super-twerp in school, could have become a best-selling author and was still a worm.

"So what have you been up to?" Loring asked. "Still fooling around writing mysteries?"

"No, I'm really too busy for that," Dooley said. "Patients, speeches, papers. You know."

"Last I heard, you'd written four or five of them," Loring said. "Hadn't sold any either."

"I write them for my own amusement," Dooley said. "When I have the free time."

"Know what the difference between a successful writer and a flop is?" Loring asked.

"No."

"That's what I thought."

Later, after Loring went off to Elaine's for lunch with his agent, Dooley walked down Fifth Avenue to consider his next move. He passed a bookstore and there was a pile of Loring's latest book in the window.

Dooley went inside and bought a copy. "He's helped me so much," the clerk said. "I read all his books."

"Swell," Dooley said.

He took the book and walked toward the East River. Paul Loring back in college, he thought, wasn't even in the top 25 percent in their class. Dooley was in the top ten.

Loring had dated Cynthia Malbry for two years, and that's all he dated. He had turned down Cynthia's advances when she flirted with him at the International Peace Rally.

Loring had been third board on the chess team. He had stood second on the debating squad. Loring always had acne. He'd smoked a pipe. He'd worn dumb sweaters.

Now he had his picture in stupid magazines with incredible circulation. He did TV talk shows. He turned away patients.

Why? All because book editors were stupid, blind, ignorant, vicious, demonic fools who kept rejecting the ingenious mysteries written by the ultimately victorious Dr. Don Dooley.

When Dooley reached the East River, he took a knife from his jacket and slashed Loring's book to shreds. Then he threw the pieces into the river and watched them float into the blackness.

Chapter 15

MELANIE ARMATRAZ WAS dusting the office plants when Anne and Brian walked into the lobby. "I have one of those writers you wanted," she said. "The unpublished kind."

"Good," Brian said. Then he turned around and saw her.

She was old, maybe 60 or 65, at that age when age itself takes over and becomes the predominant physical feature. She had all the looks that go with age and no money: the dried skin, the gray hair pulled back and held with a green rubber band, the kind used on newspapers. Her thready coat opened over a flowered dress whose roses had turned gray. She held a shopping bag on her lap.

As she stood up, her body bent in too many places: stooped shoulders, knotted back, bowed legs, making her look heavy and frail at the same time. Brian's mother was starting to look like that, which was one reason he only saw her once a year.

The old woman reached into her shopping bag and pulled out a cardboard box tied with string. "My book," she said. "Read it, please." Her voice was raspy and breathless, the kind of voice Brian had heard in emergency rooms from people who weren't going to make it.

"We encourage writers to mail in their books," Anne said.

"I know, dear," the woman said. "But at my age I can't wait around for the post office."

"We'll read your book as soon as we can," Brian said. He took the box from her.

"Today?"

"Soon."

The old woman nodded and limped to the door. "I'll be in all day. And tomorrow. I hope." She reached for the door knob, missed, and stumbled. Brian caught her and moved toward a chair.

"Inside," she said. "There's such a draft out here."

"Shall we call an ambulance?" Anne asked.

"There's nothing the doctors can do for me any more," the old woman said. "If I could just sit for a moment."

Brian walked her back into Anne's office and helped her into a chair, while Anne scowled.

"A sip of brandy might help," the old woman said.

Anne got a bottle of Remy Martin from a file cabinet. The old woman sipped slowly. "Ah, that's better," she said. "A little."

Brian looked at the top of the cardboard box, where the woman had hand-lettered: *That Old Gang of Mine,* a mystery novel by Eleanor Parker.

"What's wrong, Mrs. Parker?" Brian asked.

"Parker's my pen name," she said. "My own name is Brigid O'Hare."

"And what exactly is wrong with you, Mrs. O'Hare?"

Brigid shrugged. "I'm dying, the doctors tell me. Well, that's got to happen, I suppose. But before I go there's one more thing I want from life, to have my book published. Is that asking too much from a hard world?"

Anne looked away. "Do you have a note from your doctor?"

"Are you this kind young man's secretary, dear?" Brigid asked.

"I'm the editor," Anne said. "He's my assistant."

"If you live long enough, you see everything," Brigid said.

"We'll be glad to consider your book," Brian said.

"It would mean so much to an old lady to get my book accepted for once," Brigid said. "I've tried so hard for so long, but no one listens to me. The doctors say it might revive me."

Anne picked up the cardboard box and looked toward the door. "We'll read it right away," she said, "as soon as you're gone."

"I could wait. I wouldn't disturb you."

"I'm afraid that's impossible," Anne said.

"Why?"

Anne threw her hands up. "I don't know why it's impossible, but it is. If we had a company policy, it would be against it, and I can't read with the author staring over my shoulder. I'm trying to be nice to you, Mrs. O'Hare. But I can't be nice to you while you're still here."

"Then I'll try to hold on for your call," Brigid said. "Do you have a mother yourself, dear?"

"How do you think I got this way?"

Brigid stood up unsteadily. Brian helped her from the room and waited in the corridor until the elevator came.

"You're a sweet boy," Brigid said. "Maybe some day you'll be an editor and you can be sweet to people when it counts."

When Brian returned to the office, Anne was sitting at her desk, breaking a pile of pencils into little pieces. "Sometimes I hate this job," she said. "It's too sad."

"Maybe." Brian got another large envelope and slipped Brigid O'Hare's cardboard box into it. He put that envelope on his desk on top of Dr. Don Dooley's envelope.

"You can't suspect that sweet, sick old lady," Anne said.

"I can't afford not to."

Brian's eyes were getting blurry from skimming so many manuscripts. The office door burst open and a tiny man sped in, himself a blur. He tossed a sketch pad on Anne's desk.

"You're the judge, you tell me," he said.

The man wore white jeans and a silk shirt with red, green, and purple fish swimming over it. He made Brian seasick.

Anne looked over at Brian. "This, in case you were wondering, is Ken Kensington, one of our art directors."

Kensington turned and raised his eyebrows at Brian. "One of, one of," he said. "I am *an* art director. I am not one of anything."

"Brian Skiles is my new assistant editor," Anne said.

"Yes, I could tell he was the inky type," Ken said. "The corduroy jacket, a dead giveaway."

In a publishing house, I'm just another editor, Brian thought. At a race track, just another gambler. On the street, a face in the crowd. Other people lead lives; detectives fake them.

Ken tapped the sketchpad on Anne's desk. "Don't keep me in suspense. Do you like the cover, or must I fall on my Exacto knife?"

Anne looked at the drawing, then showed it to Brian. "Another brilliant design," she said. "But did you happen to read the book summary I sent around before you conceived the cover?"

"I always read them," Ken said, "right down to the last nasty little word."

"Because in your cover design here, you have a chef cooking mushrooms," Anne said. "Wouldn't you agree?"

"Does this conversation have some point to it?" Ken crossed in front of Anne's desk, picked up the sketchpad, crossed back and put it down on the desk again.

"Always a tough question," Anne admitted. "But the point is, the book is a whodunit, you see? In the mystery business, that means the reader wants to guess who the killer is, or try. And if the book is done right, the reader doesn't figure it out until the last page."

"What fun."

"Perhaps not," Anne said. "You see, in this book, *No Stomach for Murder,* the killer turns out to be the chef. And he does his victims in by slipping poison mushrooms into their food."

"Life is full of tragedy."

"Not the least of which is that you give away the entire solution to the mystery on your cover."

"Don't be so literal. No one will notice." Ken picked up the sketchpad again, crossed the desk, and put it back down. He turned it around, looked at it and turned it back. "People don't judge books by the cover, you know."

"Let's humor me and try something else," Anne said. "How about a nice naked woman?"

"I'm so tired of naked women," Ken sighed. "That's all I ever see around here. I've done naked women from the front, from the back, and upside down. I've done them in bed, after bed, on the balcony, on the floor. Peeking out of fur coats and velvet dresses and even a suit of armor. Surely there must be something your lust-driven readers care about besides a naked woman?"

"How about two naked women?" Brian suggested.

Ken studied Brian with a fierce glare. He picked up the sketchpad and advanced on Brian's desk. "Two naked women? Yes, a breakthrough in book design. A revolutionary concept. I'll put it on the drawing board and see if anything comes up." He jabbed at the sketchpad with a pencil, spun on his heel, and left the room.

"Well, Mr. Skiles," Anne said. "You're an editor now."

Chapter 16

BRIGID O'HARE TRIED not to listen to what Mr. Clements was saying. But since everyone else in the writing class was listening to him, there wasn't anything else to do.

"My father had hands like vise grips," Mr. Clements read, "from his years working in the mill. And his mind had been forged by the same fire that blackened his hands, so when he laid down the law in our house, you knew it had been set in steel."

Who cares? Brigid thought. Anyone could work in a mill. All you needed was the job. Anyone could have a father who was a bastard. You could hardly find any other kind.

So why did all these wheezebags waste so much time writing about how fondly they remembered their fathers and mothers who made their youth so miserable and their old age so obsessed with their youth?

It was the fourth story read this morning in the West Side Senior Center's writing workshop about someone's memories of the good old days. If the good old days were so good, Brigid wondered, why had they led to so many bad new ones?

She looked around the square of tables at the dozen people in their sixties and seventies and shook her head. The only young person in the group was the teacher, who at 30 supported his own dreams of becoming a writer by leading workshops that made other people who would never become writers think they could.

Mr. Clements wouldn't stop. "And so when I hear young people today say they don't like their fathers," he droned on, "I think of mine and how he would have taught them the law of steel: before you can criticize someone else, you have to test their metal."

As Mr. Clements finished the story, he looked up at the class expectantly. The 12 seniors applauded warmly. Brigid applauded too because the class had once spent 15 minutes discussing why she didn't applaud like everyone else. But she didn't do it warmly. Brigid was sick of this memory writing, this nostalgia for common lives and ordinary events.

"I think we can see once again," the teacher said, "how well all of you can write when you're writing from the truth of your own experiences."

He wasn't looking at Brigid when he said that, but she knew he was talking to her. "We see how the metaphors and the meaning flow naturally like maple from the tree of your real lives."

The class spent 10 minutes agreeing with the teacher that Mr. Clements was one wonderful rememberer and a heck of a good writer. They all were, according to them, wonderful writers. Even though none of them had ever been published. Not for real anyway.

Three of them had their memory stories published in the senior center's newsletter, but Brigid didn't count that because the newsletter published anything anyone wrote as long as it had enough paper. Besides, no one else read it but other wheezebags.

Mrs. Greenburg had written a novel based on her experiences as a bookkeeper in Queens. She had read six excruciating chapters to the class. All the publishers had turned the book down, of course, as the class should have after chapter one. But they were committed to being supportive of each other, which Brigid knew meant: I'll lie about yours if you'll lie about mine.

Then Mrs. Greenburg had used some of her husband's investment revenue to have her book printed. Everyone in the class had been forced to buy a copy. As time went by, they forgot that Mrs. Greenburg had paid for it herself, which was not publishing but printing, and called her "our own published novelist."

Brigid didn't forget. Although she admitted that if Mrs. Greenburg went to enough workshops for unpublished writers and forced all of them to buy copies of her book, she could become a best-seller.

But that didn't make her a real writer. Only a real publisher could do that. One that paid money for your book, acknowledged its importance, and put it in the window of real bookstores.

So far, Brigid had written three books about gangsters, and all of them had been rejected. By the real publishers. And even more infuriating, by the fools in her writing workshop at the senior center.

You have to write about what you know, they all told her, assuming she didn't know anything about gangsters because gangsters and little old white-haired ladies didn't mix. They all thought she was just a crazy lady who had seen too much TV and was making up fantasies because she couldn't remember her own memories. They didn't realize that she had to write her stories as fiction because if she used real names real people would not like that.

That's why when the teacher, frustrated with her refusal to write the same boring family memories as everyone else in the class, had asked her point-blank if she were making up the stories, she had to admit that she was. She had to say that to protect herself. For gangsters, there was no statute of limitations on squealing. And Brigid was a story teller, not a squealer.

"So where can I get this story published?" Mr. Clements asked when everyone was through telling him how wonderful he was and how his memories reminded them of their own memories, which they would be sure to write up for the next class. It was the question they all asked the teacher, always, and the one he had never answered to anyone's satisfaction.

"Well, what does the class think would be a good place?" the teacher said.

I know what I think, Brigid thought. I think you have never had anything published either. Which wasn't exactly true, since he had sold to the class 14 copies of the obscure literary magazine that had published one of his short stories.

"*Reader's Digest* would be perfect," someone suggested.

But someone thought *Reader's Digest* was perfect for every story they wrote (except Brigid's, of course), although none of the editors at *Reader's Digest* ever agreed with them.

The class also liked the *Saturday Evening Post, Redbook,* and *TV Guide,* none of which had ever bought anything everyone thought they should, although these magazines published plenty of stories the class agreed were not nearly as good as their own.

"How about you, Mrs. O'Hare?" the teacher asked. "We haven't heard from you yet. Do you have a story for us?"

"This one's called, 'The Bank Heist,' " Brigid said, opening her folder.

"Mrs. O'Hare," the teacher interrupted, proving that his manners were as bad as his story judgment, "when are you going to listen to the class? When are you going to give us something real, something true?"

I'd like to give you something real, Brigid thought. A slug in the guts. I believe that would give you all something to remember.

Chapter 17

THE PILE ON THE right side of Brian's desk was slowly rising, while the unread manuscripts were steadily diminishing. He felt like he was back in school, cramming for a test in a subject he was never going to use later in life, like algebra or ancient history.

Anne sat across the office, proofing typeset galleys.

The door opened. Brian looked up in relief, then he saw the suntanned face of the publisher, Brandon Everall, and thought that situations didn't necessarily improve just because they changed.

Brandon looked windswept, as if he'd stepped off a sailboat instead of an elevator. "Catch anything yet?" he asked.

Anne looked up from the galleys. "Three typos and a dangling participle. But no killers, if that's what you mean."

"How about you, Skiles, keeping busy?" Brandon asked.

"I'm here to do a job," Brian said.

"Personally," Brandon said, "I like a man who is so totally devoted to his work that he doesn't have time for anything else, like romance and other trivial pursuits."

"If you're looking for romance," Anne said, "you're in the wrong department. Romance is down the hall. In the Mystery Department, the bodies do pile up but not on top of each other."

"Yes, I see." Brandon picked up a manuscript, thumbed it, then put it down as if the pages had contained something he didn't want to get on his hands.

"Did you actually want something, Brandon?" Anne asked. "Or are you here to make sure we're not rolling around on top of the desks?"

"Only wanted to see if I could be of any help," Brandon said.

"Sure," Anne answered. "Double my salary and get me a submachine gun."

"That's what I love about you, Anne," Brandon said, "always kidding. Not a serious bone in her body, eh Brian?"

"I haven't gotten to her bones yet," Brian said.

"Not a serious muscle in her body either," Brandon said. "Not a ligament, not a serious organ."

"Leave my organs out of this," Anne said.

"I know there's something going on between you," Brandon said.

"There's nothing between us," Brian said. "She doesn't like me, and I don't like her. Together, there's nothing we like."

"That's what people always say right before they fall in love," Brandon said.

Brian put his notebook inside his jacket and picked up the envelopes containing the manuscripts from Dr. Don Dooley and Brigid O'Hare. He headed for the door.

"I'm taking these down to the lab for prints," he said. "No one at a police station ever accuses you of loving anyone."

* * *

An hour later, Anne was reviewing production schedules when Brian's ex-wife Cathy came into her office.

"That cute little receptionist said it was okay to come back," Cathy said. "You're not busy with anything important, are you?"

"Just work," Anne said.

"I need your help. There's something I must tell Brian, but I've been putting it off. Then when I saw him with you, I told myself that a complete woman would not put it off any longer but would do what had to be done. But I couldn't do it. I felt that thing happen in my heart."

"Gas?"

"Love. That's when I realized that I had to give Brian another chance. I owe it to myself."

"What exactly are you giving Brian a chance at?" Anne asked.

"I'm thinking of getting married again."

"To Brian?"

"Please, try to contain your natural instinct to misunderstand me," Cathy said. "Hank has asked me to marry him, and Hank is not a man to be taken lightly."

"No," Anne said. "Exactly who is Hank?"

"Captain Henry Stark," Cathy said. "Brian's boss, his former partner."

"The one with the glass jaw?"

"If you are referring to that unfortunate incident the TV stations keep exploiting when a suspect took him by surprise, it was entirely irrelevant to Hank's future as a law enforcement administrator. Hank is going to be very big in the police department."

"Only if he starts taking his vitamins," Anne said. "Which I'm sure he will if you marry him."

"Marrying Hank would be good for me," Cathy said. "But I couldn't marry Hank if Brian still loved me."

"I know this is a dumb question," Anne said, "but if you love Brian, why did you leave him?"

"He was easier to love than to live with," Cathy said. "I'm not the kind of wife who can be second in her man's heart."

The phone rang, which Anne thought was terribly bad timing, as it seemed certain she was about to learn some good dirt on Brian. She picked up the phone and said, "What?"

"Anne, it's Brian."

"I'm not at all surprised."

"Listen, I'm following a lead and I won't be coming back to the office tonight. You're not going to work alone?"

"I'm not alone."

"Are you with someone you can trust?"

Anne laughed. "That's an interesting question."

"Anne, I'm serious. Don't play with killers."

"I'm fine, really. You go follow up your lead, and I'll see you tomorrow."

"Why didn't you tell him I was here with you?" Cathy asked when Anne hung up.

"Because you were about to tell me how he was cheating on you."

"He was cheating on me," Cathy said. "But not with another woman. I'm not the kind of woman who has to worry about other women."

"Yes, I noticed."

"It was his job. Catching bad guys meant more to him than I did. Being a detective isn't a career with him. It's a quest."

"Why?"

"He hasn't told you about his father?"

"Not yet."

"Maybe I shouldn't either," Cathy said. "But that's never stopped me. When Brian was a kid, his father was murdered."

"Oh."

"Exactly. His father was a lawyer. They found him shot in his officc one night. The police never caught the killer."

"And that's why Brian's so passionate about catching murderers."

"Maybe he thinks it will bring his father back somehow," Cathy said. "You know how men are, don't you?"

"Poor Brian."

"That's the way I felt for a long time," Cathy said. "But I needed Brian to succeed and he couldn't do that for me."

"I thought Brian was a good detective."

"He can catch crooks," Cathy said. "But he hasn't gotten anywhere in the department. He wouldn't play departmental politics. Never went to lunch with the right people, never joined the right clubs. All he did was his job. You can't get anywhere like that. Look at Hank, not half the detective Brian is and he's made captain already."

"Can I ask you something personal?" Anne asked.

"No, I didn't fool around with Hank when I was married to Brian," Cathy said. "That came after we broke up. But Hank was Brian's partner, so when I went for him, I didn't have far to go."

"This is quite fascinating," Anne said. "But why tell me?"

"If Brian still loves me, then I won't marry Hank."

"Then why don't you tell him how you feel?"

"I couldn't do that," Cathy said. "But you could."

"Me?"

"He loves me too much to tell me how he really feels about me. But he doesn't like you, so he'll tell you."

"This is crazy."

"Maybe, but it's important. If Brian doesn't come back to me, he'll have to quit the police force."

"I'm glad I didn't major in logic," Anne said. "You want to explain it to me anyway?"

"If Brian doesn't come back to me, then I'm going to marry Hank," Cathy said. "But not if Brian is still on the force. It's a matter of principle. Hank can't marry another cop's wife, and still become police commissioner. But if Brian is no longer on the force, then Hank and I can get married and it won't affect his job."

"Brian won't quit for that."

"One way or another, he'll be out," Cathy said. "Hank's good at that kind of thing."

Chapter 18

"Good of you to see me on such short notice," Brian said. "I know it's late."

"I often work late hours," Dr. Don Dooley said. "It comes with the job." He led Brian through the small reception room. "Problems don't always give people advance notice. Psychiatrists must expect the same from the people they help."

Dooley settled behind his desk in an office sedately painted in muted grays, with his framed degrees on the walls. He motioned Brian into a leather chair facing his desk.

"However, I must confess that when you called me," Dooley continued, "I thought it was to accept my book for publication."

"That's part of my problem," Brian said. "I like your book. It's exactly the kind of book we should be publishing at Everall."

Dooley leaned forward across his desk and clasped his hands. "That's good to hear. I need more patients like you. I don't know if I can solve your problems, but you can definitely solve mine."

"The problem is we haven't gotten to the problem yet."

"But you like my detective—the psychiatrist? Other detectives can solve crimes," Dooley said. "But he understands *why* people commit them."

"No problem there," Brian said.

"We can work out the details later. Tell me about the deal." Dooley leaned forward, and Brian thought he might pitch headfirst across the desk.

"That's the problem," Brian said. "As an assistant editor, I don't have the authority to purchase books like yours. I can recommend them to the people above me, but my recommendations don't carry enough weight."

"What about your boss, this Anne Baker?" Dooley folded his arms across his chest. "Doesn't she feel the way you do about the book?"

"I'm afraid not," Brian said. "Although she hasn't made her final decision yet, it doesn't look all that promising."

Dooley stood up sharply, began to pace from wall to wall. "Perhaps you could reason with her. Find a way to overcome her objections to buying the book."

"I've been through this before too many times," Brian said. "It's a power trip with her. She's worried that if she publishes your book on my recommendation, I'll get the credit and people will think I'm better than she is. That scares her."

"Perhaps she needs counseling more than you do."

"I'm sure you're right," Brian said. "But I couldn't get her to come here. Meanwhile, I've been up for promotions four times, but I've been rejected each time in favor of people who aren't half the editor I am. It's getting to me, all this rejection. When I heard you talking about how to handle rejection, I thought maybe you could help me."

Dooley paced silently for a moment. Then he sat down and looked across the desk at Brian. "Psychiatry is not a Band-Aid. If I'm to help you, we would have to explore your childhood, where these patterns of rejection and resentment are formed. This would take many years. But what if your immediate problem was not your fault? It's the old psychiatric conundrum: simply because a man is paranoid doesn't mean he isn't being followed."

"I'm not sure I follow you."

"Exactly. Look, you resent working for people inferior to yourself. Since your superiority has not been recognized, you blame yourself for having failed. But perhaps you are not to blame. If the people above you are truly inferior, then they would be incapable of recognizing your superiority."

"But what can I do about it?"

"That's always the trick, what to do about it," Dooley said. "You must use your superiority to overcome their inferiority. It's no easy task. Inferiority is a powerful weapon. So you must be clever, learn to break the rules of the inferior people."

"Has it worked for you?" Brian asked.

"We'll see," Dooley said.

Chapter 19

IT WAS DARK when the cab stopped in front of Anne's apartment house. Alonzo, the night doorman, came out to escort Anne in because she was such a lonely lady—never had men stay overnight—and she tipped so well.

The electronic timers had lit her apartment, and the automatic microwave had thawed her frozen chicken. In the bedroom she threw her clothes in the closet, put on her favorite jeans and faded denim shirt, and went out to the living room.

Anne poured a glass of red wine, switched on all three TV sets, and sat down behind her typewriter, wondering if she should write a chapter on Brian Skiles' wife. The problem was Anne didn't know if Cathy McDougald would affect the case, although it was obvious she affected Brian.

And me, Anne thought. They've made me their go-between. I've become a crimeless victim. First, Brian puts me between him and the killer. Now, between him and his wife.

Of course, better their affair than one of my own, Anne thought. It was a freeing sensation to be manless, to unburden yourself from the weight of men. It left you free to think, to work, to focus on what really mattered.

People wanted to fall in love, but what they fell into was a mess. I love you, but you love someone else. I can't trust you. I can't trust me. Can't live with you. Can't live without you.

If I was in love, Anne thought, I would be waiting for him to come home, wondering where he was, what he was doing, who he was doing it with. Instead, I'm free to kick off my shoes, have a glass of wine without wondering where it will lead, and get to work on the book that is going to make me rich and famous.

The microwave bell rang, but Anne wasn't hungry any more. What she really wanted to do was write. So she did.

Once you got rid of men, there was nothing to stop you from getting rid of all your other obligations, nothing standing in the way of total freedom. She typed, "Chapter Four."

When Brian got home, he washed the mushrooms he had picked up at the corner store and put them into the crock pot, where a stew, simmering all day was starting to get interesting.

Brian added wine and a cup of lentils to the stew, which already contained beef, sausages, red potatoes, yellow split peas, onions, garlic, carrots, and celery root.

He liked to cook that way, putting everything he had into the pot and feeding off the results.

While the lentils and mushrooms were cooking down, he opened a beer and checked on his forest mural. The fox peered out at the bleak spring from under a juniper bush. He picked up a pencil and sketched a wolf standing behind the boulders where the snow had melted last week. The wolf was watching the fox. Who was watching the wolves?

The phone rang. "Brian Skiles."

"Hello, Brian," a woman said. "It's Deirdre Bolling. From Boston."

"Hello, Deirdre."

"I have to shuttle down to New York on business tomorrow. I'd like to get together with you after my meeting, say about seven."

"I can't, Deirdre."

"Brian, I'm only going to be in town for the one night."

"Sorry. Not this time."

"You have someone else?"

"No."

"Then what?"

"I'm busy on a case."

"No one works all the time," Deirdre said, her voice tightening. "No one works night and day, twenty-four hours."

"It's different with me."

"But I look forward to our sordid little rendezvous when I come to New York. It's the one excitement I allow myself."

"Sorry, I can't do it."

"Then do you know someone else who can? Someone safe and discreet and good enough to make it worth my time?"

"I'm not running a service here for busy businesswomen."

"That's exactly what you've been doing, Brian. Providing a service. But people don't stop shopping just because you close up shop."

"Deirdre, it's been swell." Brian hung up. He looked at his painting for a long time, then went into the kitchen and stirred the stew.

Women, Brian thought, always came at you from the strangest trajectory. Like Cathy. Gone for years, then she shows up in the wrong place at the wrong time. She wanted something from him, because she didn't do anything unless it was to get something she wanted.

He had met Cathy along a strange trajectory. He had joined her health club because he suspected that a rapist-killer scouted at the club. He never found the killer, but he did find Cathy.

She taught aerobics classes. They liked each other right away, the one time in his life when he saw sparks and recognized them for what they were.

The first time Cathy took him back to her apartment, she stole his gun. They were drinking wine and listening to Steely Dan. Halfway through the bottle, he took off his jacket and shoulder holster and draped them over a chair.

They drank and talked and watched each other, knowing what would happen, enjoying the tension created by the delay. She sent him into the kitchen for a second bottle of wine.

When he came back, she was pointing the gun at him.

"Take off your clothes," she said.

He looked at her and the gun and couldn't tell if he was about to do something thrilling or had fallen into a lunatic's trap.

That night he had the most intense sexual experiences of his life. For the next four months, he kept after Cathy until she married him. But after two years of marriage, he still wasn't sure what he had.

Now he wasn't sure what he had lost. But losing was safer. No sparks, maybe, but no burns either.

That was one reason he liked Anne Baker. She didn't want him any more than he didn't want her.

The phone rang. Maybe all my out-of-town women will call tonight, he thought, and I can turn them all down and they'll all get mad at me and clean my slate.

He picked up the phone. "Brian Skiles."

"Hey, Bry."

"Hey, Billy." Brian knew if his brother was calling him, there was a trade show coming up, but he couldn't remember which one it was. "It's this week, isn't it?"

"I'll be in New York tomorrow," Billy Skiles said. "I hope you'll come to the show with me. This is the biggest electronic novelties show of the year. You'll see stuff they don't even have on the Saturday morning cartoons yet."

"Can't do the show, Billy. But you come up here tomorrow night and I'll cook you dinner."

"No, I can get stew in Indiana," Billy said. "Can hardly avoid it. When I come to New York, I want to eat something covered with sauce cooked by a guy calling himself Pierre or Raoul."

"Everything okay with the kids, Marcia?"

"They're great, Bry. I'm nuts, but they're fine. You know, some days I come home from killing myself for the company and I wonder why I do it. Then one of the girls gives me a kiss, not because I've done anything but because I'm there. And I'm ready to go back out and take on the world. Always makes me wonder about single guys like you, Bry. What makes you go back out there day after day and take on the world?"

Chapter 20

BOOGIE JOHN WAS DEAD. The Sheik was dead. Big Eddie Little was dead; God, the way that man could eat. Zadie Z. and his kid brother Allie were both dead, funny guys but dangerous with knives.

Of all the guys Brigid O'Hare had known, the guys who had given her stones off the top of a heist, the guys who had taken her for rides in hot cars, the guys she had lived with, fought with, married—nearly all of them were dead.

Safer that way, she thought. Most of them were so crazy, the only safe place for them was in her memories.

Brigid got the Old Overholt from the shelf and sat down at the typing table. She moved without the limp she had used on the editors, and several of the age lines were gone from her face.

But Brigid still felt old, even if that didn't always raise sympathy in an editor's cold heart. Everything in Brigid's apartment was old: old table, old chairs, old bed, even the walls were old. The pieces of her life were slipping, like a jigsaw puzzle that was so old the locking edges had worn down.

Brigid sat at the typing table and poured herself a shot. The clock on the wall said three. Out the window, the sky was black, which made it three in the morning. She turned back to the typewriter, reading the words she had started at sundown:

"Maggie was old, but she had once been young and she had lived in the neighborhood all her long life and knew everyone who lived there, long or short, and what they did and what they didn't want other people to know they did. And that's why people came to her when they had bad problems, trouble the cops couldn't do anything about or the mob bosses wouldn't.

"Maggie helped them because when she was young she had been bad, but at her age the only thing left she could do was be good."

Brigid read the words twice. Then she pulled a beer from the pail of ice beside the table and typed: "People came to her because she was good at figuring out bad things. People like Bill Bartkowski, whose brother Ned, the lawyer, had disappeared a year ago."

Brigid sipped some of the rye and thought about Leather Phil. Phil Petowski, the lawyer who had defended Brigid and many of her friends. Phil Petowski, with his old leather briefcase, who had disappeared from the neighborhood one night and was never seen again. Some people said the mob took him out, but they weren't people who knew anything. Brigid figured Leather Phil left voluntarily because he couldn't stand the people he spent his life trying to get off for all the crimes they committed.

People like Phil's cousin, Joe Forty-five, the son of a cop and the best shot Brigid had ever seen, although not much as a lover. Joe Forty-five was a hired killer for the Irish mob. His specialty was shooting people when they were moving past in a car and he was standing in a doorway. Joe was gunned down by cops in a bank heist he tried to pull by himself, imitating the one he had worked on for the Professor, but without the Professor's talents.

The Professor, everyone agreed, was the smartest bank robber on the east coast when it came to planning a job. But he was also stupid because he had to prove how smart he was, which he could only do by telling people what he had done. Eventually, someone would snitch on him, and the Professor would go off to prison, where at least he had a good audience, although he died in the last one.

Which broke May's heart, although no one knew that May and the Professor had a thing going; that was one secret he had been able to keep. May Dineer had been Brigid's best friend when they both worked tables at Lawry's Place on the West Side. They stayed friends even though May married someone from the Green Gang and Brigid married Country Kelser, her second husband, who was from Big Shoulders' gang. But Brigid had to give up on May when she began stealing from her friends so she could afford to be a junkie. May ended up dying in the explosion when Fat Green tried to make bombs in his bedroom for an extortion plot after his gang broke up, which left Pecs without a leader.

Pecs, her third husband, was always lifting weights, did 1,000 situps a day, could never sit still, always lifting, squeezing, pumping. A great lover when he could find the time. Pecs was killed in a gun battle with the Bratz Brothers because he had fooled around with their younger sister, Sissy. Tommy and Danny Bratz walked into the U.S. Cafe and started shooting at Pecs without warning. They were both lousy shots, nervous too about what Pecs could do to them if they missed, and they missed. But down the bar was a hood named Falma who thought the Bratz Brothers were shooting at him because he had fooled around with Sissy too. Falma started shooting back at the Bratz Brothers, but he missed too and shot Pecs, who didn't know which way to duck.

Pecs was her last husband. Dead now, they were all dead now. Yet they lived on inside Brigid. Always with her in the empty morning hours when she couldn't sleep. They had come to her years ago, the voices demanding that she do something for them, that since she was alive she had to keep them alive. Other people had voices living inside them and it drove them nuts. But Brigid's voices belong to a tougher gang. They weren't letting her off so easy.

Brigid read a lot of books because she didn't like to go out, since none of the people she used to go out to see were there to be seen any more. From reading she saw that writers let their voices live through books. Since the people inside her mind were as real as the people in books, all she had to do was let them into the world by writing their stories.

She didn't realize when she started that the gang didn't simply want to be written about. They also wanted to be read, which meant she had to get their books published, which turned out to be another story altogether.

Brigid's first two books had been rejected over and over again until she lost count of the people who had said no. She could live with that; people were always saying no to old ladies. But it frustrated the gang inside her.

They weren't people who gave up on what they wanted, which meant the editors would have to publish Brigid's books sooner or later. There were too many people behind her, tough people, for the editors to hold out. The old gang was back, and they would come out on top or die trying, like everything else they ever did.

Do or die. That was the rule they all lived by, and it had worked for them: sometimes they did and sometimes they died. Except for Brigid. She neither did nor died.

Brigid came out of her reverie, not sure where she was. Then she saw her hands and remembered that she was old. It all came back to her after that. She reached for the bottle and looked at the clock. It was 4:30 and the sky was beginning to lighten. She looked at the paper in the typewriter. She drank some beer, warm now, and typed:

"Ned Bartkowski, the lawyer, had disappeared because he knew too much."

Maybe Leather Phil Petowski had known too much, she thought. If you lived long enough, you had to know too much.

Chapter 21

WHEN ANNE CAME OUT of the women's room, Phil Enders grabbed her arm and led her down the hall to his office. "Got a minute?" he asked. "Good."

Phil was a short, blocky man with red hair and a red face and a habit of wearing jackets with too many colors in them. He was Everall Publishing's director of sales.

His office was littered with books, piled on two credenzas, six chairs, and on the floor, everywhere but on his desk. On the walls were complex sales charts with lines going off in every direction.

Anne had once tried to decipher Phil's charts, but she had not made that mistake twice.

Phil pulled some books off a chair and didn't let go of her arm until she was sitting down. Then he hoisted a leg up on the corner of his desk and leaned over her.

"You're asking for a big press run on this new book, *Death Makes the Grade,*" he said. "The one about the lady English professor who solves crimes when she's not lecturing everyone."

"I'm familiar with the book," Anne said.

"Then maybe you can tell me how I'm supposed to sell twenty thousand copies," Phil said. "This professor, she doesn't even have legs that won't quit or a body like the sun-ripened fruit of the gods. What kind of a woman is this?"

"She's a professor."

"I'm getting to that," Phil said. "But first, she doesn't go to bed with anyone for two hundred pages; and when she does, no stars explode, no magic moments, not a single metaphor. What am I supposed to do with that?"

"Are you having a problem with this book?" Anne edged her chair backward, and Phil leaned forward.

"Let's face the truth about this English professor: she's flatchested. Has to be. That's why the author didn't write about her chest. If she was world-class, she would have mentioned it. They always do. Am I right?"

"Have you ever been?"

"So if she's flatchested, she must be a lesbian. Am I right?"

"Are you trying to tell me that a small chest makes you gay?" Anne pushed her chair back another inch. Phil inched forward on the desk. She was hoping she could make him fall off.

"In books," he said. "I don't know anything about real life. That's not my territory. I sell books. Now maybe there have been one or two books with flat women who weren't gay, but how much did they sell? Now this English professor, she's smart, right?"

"Not necessarily," Anne said. "Maybe she has tenure."

Phil started pacing behind her. She turned to keep an eye on him.

"Anyway if she is smart, she is going to be gay and I'll tell you why," Phil said. "It's smart, in general, to like women. It's stupid to like men. You see how it works?"

"In books?"

"Wrong, in real life. In books, who cares? I have to sell these things in real life, don't I?"

Phil stopped pacing, and Anne stood up. "I'm sure you're leading up to something, but I'm not sure I can stay here long enough to find out what."

Phil moved to the office door and put his back against it. "The point is if this English professor detective with the chest made in Kansas is gay like the rules of writing say she has to be, then the solution to the murder is all wrong. Am I right?"

Anne sat down again. "I shudder to think," she said.

"The lawyer couldn't have done it," Phil explained. "He's not a threatening male figure. The killer has to be the dean of the psychology department. It's Freudian, you see. It always is. Am I right?"

"Let's avoid the entire issue of whether or not you're right as something that could shatter the fabric of the universe as we know it," Anne said. "And let me plunge right into asking you, with much trepidation, what the hell do you want me to do about it?"

"I thought you'd never ask." Phil pulled a chair close to Anne and sat down on top of two books. "I want you to get the author to make the dean the killer or give the professor a chest, either way I'll sell ten thousand more copies."

"Why don't I give you the author's phone number and you can tell her exactly what you have in mind yourself. I'll listen in on the other phone, just for sport."

Phil shook his head. "No, I don't want to interfere in the editorial process. That's not my job. I only want to sell more books. You help me, and I'll help you."

"How can you help me?"

Phil leaned back in his chair. "I can leave you alone for a week, maybe two. And I can keep your sales figures from flattening out. Wouldn't you rather be known as the editor of a book about a professor with the body of sun-ripened fruit that sold twenty thousand copies than the book about a real woman that sold ten thousand copies? To me the choice is obvious, but I leave it up to you."

Brian had taken off his overcoat in the elevator, but as he entered Anne's office, he put it back on again.

"It's freezing in here," he said.

"If it's Thursday, the heater must be on the fritz." Anne wore a white turtleneck sweater over her blouse and had pulled the neck up over her chin. She was editing two chapters of their book she had finished last night.

"Doesn't anything ever work in this place?" Brian tossed his overcoat on a chair and buttoned his suit jacket.

"Just me."

"Why do you do it? With your brains, you could get a better job."

"It's the books," Anne said. "They let me make books. Maybe some of them will outlive me."

The heater in Melanie Armatraz's reception lobby was working fine because she would have quit if it didn't, and it was easier for Brandon Everall to have that heater fixed than find another receptionist. With editors, it was just the opposite.

Melanie was reading the latest science fiction novel published by Everall, although it wasn't the kind of SF she would have published because it was dull.

However, the guy who came through the door was anything but dull. He was young, tall, and handsome. Melanie felt sure that he was a writer, one of the unpublished kind. She had seen enough of them to recognize the signs. But he looked like the kind of guy that Hollywood would cast as a writer, not the kind who were forced to become a writer by their brains.

"I want to see your mystery editor," he said, "and I won't take no for an answer." He wore a leather jacket and gloves and had thick, dark hair with a ringlet that fell across his forehead. He carried a cardboard box tied with string.

"Will you take yes?" Melanie asked.

His mouth fell open as he stared at her suspiciously. Good teeth, Melanie thought, white with some bite.

"What do you mean yes?" he asked.

"What do you think it means?" For Melanie, this was the first time that Anne Baker's order to let unpublished writers go back made any sense. "First door on your left." She pointed down the hall. He looked at her like she was playing a joke on him. "What's your name?"

"Rep Gates. I know I don't have an appointment . . ."

"Mine's Melanie. First door on your left."

He rolled his shoulders and set his mouth like a man determined to see a bad joke through to the end. Then he wheeled about and walked off down the hall.

Melanie watched him go. Good bod, she thought. She turned back to her desk, and her eye was caught by a report one of the assistant editors in How-to had asked her to type.

Melanie hated typing even more than she hated filing, collating, or distributing. The way she saw it, work was something adults did to punish kids for growing up. She hated the waste of time work demanded, trying to satisfy other people when that was impossible anyway. She preferred to read fantasy books and sleep with interesting men.

She had chosen to be a receptionist despite the low pay because there was little work involved, which left her lots of time for her fantasies. There were plenty of receptionist jobs in New York for a good-looking young woman, and in four years she had gone through ten of them. She always quit when they asked her to type or file or sleep with old, fat executives.

When she went to work for Everall Publishing, she found the perfect receptionist's job because they didn't mind her reading books at work, as long as it was their books she read. Most of the editors were women so she wasn't being pestered for sex all the time. Best of all, the writers who came through her lobby were perfect fantasy lovers because they lived in a fantasy world.

Hmmm, Rep Gates, she thought.

Rep Gates stood outside the door marked Mystery Division and took a deep breath. Then he pushed the door open and went inside. It's freezing in here, he thought.

Rep looked around the office at the skinny woman in the turtleneck and the average-looking guy in the cord jacket. "Who's the boss here?" he asked.

The woman gave him one of those smirky smiles that smart women always give guys they think are too handsome for them but not smart enough. "My name is Anne Baker," she said. "This is my assistant, Brian Skiles. What can we do for you?"

"Not as much as I can do for you," Rep said. "I've got a book that's going to be big. There's only one question: Is it going to be big for you or for someone else?" Rep was satisfied that he had gotten it all out the way he had memorized it over the past two days.

"Have you been published before?" Brian asked.

Now it was coming, Rep thought, now he was going to get the old brush-off. "What difference does that make? I'm talking about a great book here." Good, just as he had rehearsed.

"It makes a lot of difference," Brian said. "We're looking for the best unpublished writer in America."

"You are?"

"Someone has to," Anne said. "Only the unpublished can qualify for our new program."

"That's me. I'm great and I'm unpublished. I'm Rep Gates."

"You're what?"

"Rep Gates. I've even got a great writer's name."

"Make yourself comfortable, Mr. Gates. Take off your stuff," Brian said.

"It's freezing in here," Rep said. He sat down by Anne's desk but kept his jacket and gloves on.

"Why do you want to be a writer?" Anne asked.

"I've done it all," Rep said, happy that he could now get back to his rehearsed speech. "Worked in factories, cowboyed on a ranch, bummed the roads. Now I tend bar in the Village, at Mac's Place. The only thing I've seriously missed so far is prison. My lawyer keeps getting me off."

"You'll have to get a lousier lawyer," Anne muttered.

"Other editors weren't smart enough to see how great my books are," Rep continued. "That's why I've come to you."

"All the great writers had their books rejected in the beginning," Anne said. "So we decided that was the best place to look for the next great writer."

"I've been rejected by the best," Rep said.

"The bigger the publisher who rejected you," Anne said, "the better the chance that you'll become a great writer."

"Other editors didn't have the vision to see how important my novel is," Rep said. "It's called *After the Big Sleep.*"

"You've written a sequel to Chandler's classic?" Anne asked.

"Not a sequel, a requel," Rep said. "Philip Marlowe gets reincarnated and becomes a detective again in 1988. He's just as tough as he was back then, but now he's in a modern world and has to relate and eat yogurt and everything we have to do. He's the first anti-antihero, a liberated tough guy. He'll still shoot a broad when he has to, but he's not afraid to relate to her first."

"You sound like the kind of writer we're looking for," Brian said.

On his way back out through the lobby, Rep Gates smiled at Melanie Armatraz. A looker, he thought, the type that melts. "This must be my day," he said.

"Could be your night too," she said.

"What do you have in mind?"

"A drink. Maybe dinner. I get off at five."

Brian looked dismally at the box containing Rep Gates' manuscript. "Odds are, we're not going to find his fingerprints on the box cover," he said. "If your heater worked, he would have taken off his gloves before he handed it over."

Anne shrugged. "Open it up and look inside. He didn't type the manuscript with gloves on."

Brian grinned. "I'll run this down to the lab and see what they can find."

"One other thing while you're out," Anne said. "You've got to sit down and talk to your wife."

"Why?"

"Because over the past four years, I've probably talked to her more than you have," Anne said.

Brian stared at her as he put on his overcoat. "I don't get it. Has Cathy been to see you?"

"Yesterday. We had a long talk."

"I'm sorry. I didn't mean for you to get involved."

"That's all right. If I ever switch to romance books, it will come in handy."

"Cathy's the kind of person who's always out to get something," Brian said. "Did she tell you what it is this time?"

"I can't tell you, Brian. It's too personal. Go see her. Ask her. Tell her how you really feel. But keep her away from me."

"Is this about her and Hank?" Brian asked.

"Yes, what are you going to do about it?"

"Nothing. Cathy and Hank can do whatever they want to."

Anne jumped up from her chair and came around the desk. "I can't believe I'm hearing this. I thought being a cop meant something to you. Now you're going to quit the force just to let your ex-partner off the hook. What kind of a man are you?"

"I don't know. Maybe you'd better tell me what you're talking about."

"They're planning to get married."

"To each other?"

"Stranger things have happened."

"Not many. But they deserve each other."

"They won't get married unless you quit the department."

"Why?"

"He thinks marrying another cop's wife would be bad for his career. And she won't marry him if you still love her."

"No."

"No, you don't love her?"

"No, I don't believe her."

"I don't know why I'm defending your ex-wife, but people do

change. Caterpillars change into butterflies, ugly ducklings become swans."

"Snakes shed their skins. She's up to something."

"You and Cathy better decide which one of you is really an ex. Is she an ex-wife or are you an ex-cop?"

Chapter 22

REP GATES STEPPED UP to the heavy punching bag that hung from a rafter in his loft. He followed a left with three right hooks and thought: Someone is killing bad drivers, and he becomes a folk hero known as the Mechanic because he cleans up the road, making it fun for people to drive again.

Rep grabbed a yellow pad and write down the idea. Moving back to the bag, he threw combinations and thought: Someone is killing dentists, and he becomes a folk hero known as the Tooth Fairy because he pulls a molar from each victim.

He wrote down that idea and pounded the bag again, thinking: Someone is killing TV weathermen, and he becomes a folk hero known as Mr. Sunshine because the more weathermen who die, the better the weather gets.

Rep hung a towel around his neck and crossed to the window, looking down at three winos on the corner who were trying to start a fire with newspapers wet from the slush.

He resented having to think up a new crime idea for each new book. Crooks didn't have to come up with new ideas every time. The same old crimes made them the same old money.

Rep turned up his heater and stood in front of it, jogging in place and thinking about crime. The room, too large for the heater to warm up much, was half the second story of a warehouse owned by a Korean businessman who let Rep live there cheap because he thought Rep would keep thieves away. Rep let Fao Kung think that, although what kept thieves away was what Kung stored in the warehouse below: exotic Korean herbs and medicinal roots that smelled foul to Western noses. One enterprising thief had stolen some anyway, a sample against future jobs, but threw it away after his friends could find no reason to sniff or smoke the stuff.

Rep's loft held a fridge, shower, and toilet along one wall, which an artist friend had helped him install. Across from that was the platform bed and a writing table built from Korean packing crates. On the wall behind the table and the punching bag were photos of Norman Mailer sparring with José Torres and Papa Hemingway clowning in the ring with Archie Moore.

Having absorbed some warmth, Rep jogged over to the bag and threw light combinations, thinking that he could out-punch Mailer or Hemingway. If only he could outwrite them.

Trying to make it as a writer, he thought, was like betting nothing but double zeroes at Vegas, only the odds weren't as good. Still, a man had to go for the long shots; that's what made him a man. Obsessions took you over the dead spots in your life.

Writing was Rep's long shot, and he was going to do whatever was necessary to get published. Perseverance was essential. That's why he was already planning his next book, while he waited for Anne Baker to make his dreams come true.

Writing a best-seller was simply a matter of putting together the right sensational crime with the right great detective. Then he'd have it. The rest was just filling in the gaps. The problem was there had already been too many detectives in too many books: tough guys with trenchcoats, smart guys with little gray cells, hard-working cops with the hearts of bloodhounds, lucky dicks who talked smart, detectives who were lawyers, rabbis, priests, monks, women, gays. He needed something new in a world where everything was old.

Out of breath, he hit the bag with his hardest right hook, pushed the bag away and went back to the window. The winos had finally gotten the fire going, lifting up the bottoms of their coats to let the warmth in.

The thing to remember, Rep thought, was that all writers had the same problems. At least, he had lived more than most writers. More women, more cities, more jobs, more adventures.

He had also learned there was a problem with having adventures: they were dangerous. When he was younger, he was careless of danger. All things came to he who flaunted it. Then he decided to become a writer because he needed a romantic identity. But writing was slow, which meant he had to slow down his life so he would have time to become a writer before the living killed him. He became a bartender because it gave him a way to see life without having to take part in it, the perfect set-up for a writer.

When he started writing, four years ago, he had a normal name, Richard Gates. But a press agent told him if he wanted to become a famous person, he needed a better reputation. "Right now, no one's heard of you," the agent explained. "That's why you're not famous. You may have done things famous people would do, but unless you get a name and a reputation, you've got nothing. Even if you haven't done anything, you can still get a rep. It's the rep itself that counts, not who you are."

Rep went back to work on the bag, thinking: Someone is killing press agents, only no one knows about it because there aren't any press agents left to tell them.

The doorbell rang. "Try it," Rep shouted.

Rick Hagerty came in carrying a paper bag. "I've had a revolutionary idea." Rick took a bottle of red wine from the bag and filled two glasses.

Rep wiped his face with the towel and sat down at his writing desk. "This any different from the one you had last week?"

"Who can remember the past?" Rick handed a glass to Rep. Tall, thin, bearded, Rick had paint on his jeans and a wild look in his eyes. He also had a good reputation in the Village as a mad artist. He did things that made great bar stories, which was basically all anyone asked of an artist. "Let us live for the present, or at least next Thursday," he said.

"What is it? I'm trying to write."

"You writers are all alike. You think it's all a matter of time. It's not. It's a matter of light."

Rep drank some wine and wiped off the last of the sweat that was cooling fast in the chilly room. "The Village is a great place for artists and writers, except there are so many artists and writers around, you can never get any work done."

"For a writer, you write too much," Rick said. "You need to get out and live more."

"I've already lived. That's all I did for the past ten years. Now I want to stop living and write."

Rick brought the wine over and filled their glasses. "Anyway, my great idea is to sneak into a museum, maybe the Met or MOMA, after it's closed for the night. . ."

"Stealing paintings is not a revolutionary idea," Rep said. "It's also not worth the risk unless you're stealing on commission for a guaranteed buyer."

"That's the beauty of my plan," Rick said. "We're not taking anything. We're giving. One of my paintings."

"You want to break into a museum and leave one of your paintings there?"

"Why should I wait for some museum director who couldn't paint the side of a barn to decide if my stuff is good enough to be hung. I paint it. I can hang it."

"What if you get caught?"

"Even better. Think of the publicity."

Rep pushed his glass away and looked at the ideas he had jotted on his yellow pad. Someone's killing painters, he thought. "I can't deal with distractions when I'm beginning a new book," he said.

"Finish the book some other time," Rick said. "I don't see publishers rushing your stuff into print."

"It so happens I'm negotiating with a major editor, and she is very interested in my work."

"Right. That's what I tell people when I come back from another damn gallery that turned me down. You going to help me or not? I want to do this while I've still got the passion for it."

"Look, I'm good for a free beer at the bar," Rep said, "and I'll pass along my women when I'm through. But I'm not risking jail time for you. I've got dreams of my own."

Rick screwed the cap back on the bottle of wine. "Suit yourself. I'll find someone else with the guts to go for it. Which reminds me, you going to Maurice's failure party tonight?"

"I'm on the bar," Rep said. "What's the party?"

"You have to come as your favorite unknown artist," Rick said. "There's a doorprize for whoever comes as the biggest flop."

Chapter 23

"WITH YOUR LOOKS, you should have been an actor," Jeanette Moss said as she focused the light to catch more of the ripple effect of Rep Gates' stomach.

"I was an actor," Rep said, tightening his chest muscles automatically under Jeanette's intense gaze. "Out in Hollywood."

Jeanette was satisfied she was seeing enough, so she picked up the brush and started on the canvas. "Which movie?"

They were in Jeanette's loft, Soho, him naked, her working. She was a regular at the bar, not bad looking, although Rep had never made it with her because it didn't do to go through all your regulars too fast. Too much note-comparing and nothing left for the dry spells.

"Actually, wasn't a movie," Rep said. "They told me to be discovered for the flicks, you have to do the theater first. So I went down to this place and of course I got the part."

"What play was it? Don't move."

"Something about these guys who have problems," Rep said. Posing, he decided, was going to be okay as long as the actual posing part didn't last too long. "Anyway, I'm at the rehearsal, and the guy in charge wants me to kiss this other guy. I have to explain to him that even though I'm in L.A. I don't do that kind of thing, because in Hollywood the guys need explanations if you're normal."

"Mmmm," Jeanette said, changing brushes.

"So the guy says I don't have to mean it. It's just in the play, it's make believe. And I have to explain to him further that anything you do in front of other guys is never make believe."

"Is that when you decided not to become an actor?"

"Sure, no one expects a writer to kiss anyone."

Actually, he had tried to be a rock star first. Since he couldn't play the guitar, he went out for lead singer. But since he couldn't sing, he decided to go for punk rock, where his kind of voice was apparently an asset. But the punk bands he tried out for didn't want him. And Rep knew why. They were very ugly guys in those bands, all afraid he would take away the groupies. Which he would have, of course. So he decided to become a writer, which was something you could do by yourself, without directors, without auditions.

"It's like that for artists too," Jeanette said. "We see things differently than other people, light, bodies, movement. It makes people afraid we're going to see them in ways they don't see themselves."

Rep knew how people saw him, how women saw him, and that was good. Rep looked good to women, and he lived up to it. That's why he did so well with women, in high school and the dumb years he spent in college before he decided to quit and become something so famous that quitting college would be romantic instead of a sign of failure.

He was just that kind of good-looking guy. Women wanted him. That's why he couldn't take being a failure at writing. It violated the natural order of things. Having women want you was the basic way you could tell who had it and who did not. And Rep Gates had it. From all kinds of women. So if he could have women, why couldn't he have his books published?

That's what he didn't understand.

Rep had seen writers in the bar, guys who already had books published. Some of them were sneaky little guys with hooded eyes who could nurse a cheap beer for an hour, watching everything that was going on without ever becoming a part of it.

Others were roaring drunks, who drank everything they could get someone else to pay for. The roaring guys did attract women, but they never came through, or so he had heard from some of the regulars in the bar. They roared in public and peeped in bed.

None of these successful writers were a match for Rep when it came to women. Put him in a room with a woman and any writer in the world, and he would be the one leaving with the woman. Hell, put him in a room with a writer and two women, and he'd leave with both of them.

So he had to succeed as a writer. Guys who had it succeeded. That was simply the way it was. If at first he encountered failure—and he had at first and at second—it was romantic ammunition for his eventual success story. Rep Gates would succeed because that was the natural order of things, the way he put right the harmony of the world.

"Is that for me?" Jeanette asked, putting down her brush.

"Huh?"

"I mean, are you just glad to see me or did you want to paint with it?"

Rep looked down and saw that he had an erection. Now where did that come from, he wondered, and immediately it was gone.

"Aw," Jeanette said.

"It was nothing," Rep said. He sat up on the couch and looked for something to put on.

"You seem confused," Jeanette said. "Maybe I could straighten it out for you."

She came around the easel, smiling at him. Sure, he thought, this is what she had wanted all along. Posing. And it was what that damn editor, Anne Baker, wanted too. Editing. Only she didn't know it. Yet.

Chapter 24

BRIAN WALKED QUICKLY through Union Square looking for an old bench jockey. Although the day was cold, there was no snow, no wind, which meant a lot of people were out.

Joggers in sweatsuits puffing steam, overbundled kids playing chase games, old people taking it one step at a time, junkies and crazies and rip-off artists moving to the beat of a different drummer—one who had no drums.

Brian spotted Max Pinole on a bench by the subway station. Max was lumpy from the bruises he'd taken as a New York City cop for 35 years. He wore old woolen cop pants under a navy peacoat. White tufts of hair stuck out from his navy watchcap. He sat on a copy of the *New York Times* reading the *Daily News.*

Max looked up as Brian approached. "The face looks familiar," he said. "But the name? Something Smiles. Byron Smiles?"

"Brian Skiles, homicide."

"Okay," Max said. "Helped you on a case, right, the year I retired. Gang murders."

"That's right," Brian said. "Old gang members paying off thirty-year debts."

"They at it again?"

"No, this is something different." Brian sat down on the bench. "Your landlady said I'd find you here."

Max nodded and put down his paper. "Woman talks too much. Charges too much, too. I'd move if it wasn't too much trouble. Like to go someplace where I didn't see too much. But then, pretty soon I will." Max's body shook, and it took a few seconds before Brian realized he was laughing.

Two teenage boys on skateboards glided past, one muttering, "Cop" as they passed. The kids wore wool gloves with the fingers removed, a style which always made Brian wonder if there were some guys going around wearing glove fingers without the gloves.

"Those skateboard kids," Max said, "they deliver dope, south of 14th Street. Faster than cars with the traffic, and they don't get ripped off so much, like they do in the subways. Subways are dangerous, you know. Hoods are scared of them."

"You report it to the narc squad?"

"Not me. I'm retired now," Max said. "I don't do anything for free. The desire runs down."

"You still giving out information?" Brian asked.

"Yeah, I still talk," Max said. "Everything else may go, but the mouth doesn't run down."

"Does the name Brigid O'Hare mean anything to you?"

"No. It's an airport, right?"

"It's the late fifties, fifty-eight, fifty-nine," Brian said. "Ten guys bust into a Brinks' garage in the Bronx while the drivers are loading up. There's a big shootout, and the gang drives off with nothing but assorted bulletholes. But they were never caught; the case was never solved."

"It was fifty-seven, eight guys, and the Brinks was in Brooklyn," Max said. "But otherwise."

"You know who did the job?"

"Sure, we always knew. It was Fat Green's gang. We could never get any proof on it, but we knew it was Fat."

"Was that popular knowledge?"

"About the job, sure. It was bannered in all the papers."

"But that Fat Green and his gang were the ones who did it; did everyone know that?"

"No, that never made the papers because we never busted them. The D.A. was up for re-election and wouldn't take a case he couldn't be sure of."

"So if someone knew that it was Fat Green, they would have had to know Fat," Brian said.

"Maybe. Or the cops who knew. Also it was around on the streets somewhat. Guys boasting about their wounds and all."

"But it never made it into print? If I was trying to research it, I wouldn't find it in the papers of that time or any books on crime that have been printed since?"

Max took a pint of rum from his peacoat. He drank, then offered some to Brian, who shook it off. "It would surprise the hell out of me if you found anything in a book on crime that actually had anything to do with anything that actually happened." He opened the bottle and drank again. "The cold, you know?"

"Think about Fat Green and his gang," Brian said. "Who was in it?"

"This a joke? Lots of guys were in lots of gangs from time to time. They didn't keep rosters like a baseball team. You can't look it up."

"Give me what you remember."

"All right, there was Fat of course," Max said. "The guy they called the Duke; I forget his real name. Hardtop Ford, Country Kelser, Babe Whitsen, Tony The Nail Abruzzo, Something Martin, wait, they called him Boogie John, Big Eddie Little, a big guy called Pecs, forget his name. Most of them worked for Fat one time or another. I'd have to think on the others."

"What about Brigid O'Hare?"

"This a woman?"

"Right."

"There weren't any women in the gang," Max said. "Not that I ever heard of. What kind of gang would that be with a woman in it?" He brought out the rum and drank again.

"But could she have hung out with the gang?"

"Oh, that's a totally different story. Certainly she could have done that."

"Well, did she?"

"How would I know? You can't expect me to remember all the women who hung around. These wise guys had as many women as movie stars, more because they didn't have the same standards."

"I'm talking about a woman who would have been around for a long time. Maybe lived with some of the guys, married some."

"You got a picture?"

"No. The department lost her mug years ago."

"What was she busted for?"

"Battery, burglary."

"I remember a tough Irish broad was married to Country Kelser, used to hold her own. But I can't remember her name. Lots of tough Irish broads around then. I wasn't too interested in their women, you know, because if you showed any interest in them, the next thing you would have is them on your doorstep. You didn't want that because you couldn't be a good cop busting hoods if you had their women in your bed all the time. Things may be different now. What do you want her for?"

"Just checking background."

"Christ, Byron, if she was around then, she's old now," Max said. "You trying to tell me you got nothing better to do than bust old ladies? I better stop spitting on the sidewalk. I don't want to spend my last days in jail."

Chapter 25

THE LIGHTS WERE LOW, the wine was red, and their thighs had actually touched five times during the entree. It was driving Melanie Armatraz wild.

Melanie pushed her plate away because she didn't like to make love on a full stomach. Especially not with someone as powerful as Rep Gates. Rep, what a fantasy name.

The only thing left on Rep's plate was the bone from his steak. Gnawed to the bone. She knew what that meant. And he had actually ordered oysters for both of them.

Rep filled her glass with chianti and asked, "So what do the cops think?"

She took a sip, taking her time, making sure her voice would come out low and sexy. "The cops think both editors were killed because of a love triangle."

"What do you think?" Rep leaned closer in the booth and their thighs touched a sixth time.

Melanie drank more wine. "I think they're cops. They read too much *National Enquirer.* There's a better rumor going around."

"Tell me," Rep said.

Try and stop me, Melanie thought. "The rumor is the editors were killed by a crazy writer because they wouldn't publish his book. Crazy, huh?"

"Crazy," Rep said. He drank wine, watching her over the glass just like they did on the soaps. "Who do they think it is? Which writer?"

"No one knows," Melanie said. "That's the thing about writers. There are thousands of them, the ones who want to be but can't make it. And no one knows who they are. I mean, I didn't even know who you were until you walked into the office."

"And now you do." Rep leaned closer.

"Now I do." Melanie couldn't wait any longer. She slid over in the booth until their thighs were touching from hip to knee.

Rep kissed Melanie until he knew he had her wrapped up. Then he broke free and asked, "What do the cops think about the killer being a crazy writer?"

Melanie finished her wine, leaving her leg where it was, next to his. She had him now. "The cops don't believe it," she said. "But I think Anne Baker does."

"Why?"

"She hired that Brian Skiles because she was scared to be in the office alone. She's worried she may be the next victim."

Chapter 26

Bill Skiles mopped up the last of the sauce whose name he couldn't remember with a crust of French bread and swallowed it down. He looked across the table at his younger brother and said, "Brian, don't make me make a speech."

"Fine with me." Brian pushed his own plate away, wondering what it was he had eaten. He liked French food, but he suspected there were things in it he wouldn't like if he knew what they were. "No speeches then."

"You've been a cop for what—eight, nine years now?" Bill began. "You've done more than your share. I want you to join me in Indiana, help me run the company. I need a partner I can trust."

"You used to lock up your baseball cards when you went away to summer camp and I stayed home." Brian grinned and emptied the wine bottle into Bill's glass.

"That was a long time ago."

"You don't need me," Brian said. "You must know someone else."

"I know lots of guys," Bill said. "That's why I don't trust them. You'd love Hillsdale. The police chief goes jogging, and he doesn't even carry a gun. What could be saner than that? We've got swimming, the golf course, a new ten-lane bowling alley, and the high school basketball team made the state quarterfinals last year."

"What else do you do for excitement?"

"I'm raising kids. I don't want life to be exciting. I want it to be safe." Bill finished the wine and started on his coffee.

"Speech finished?"

"Yeah."

"Same speech, same answer," Brian said. "I appreciate the offer, but I have a job to do here. I can't quit."

Bill picked up a spoon and stirred his coffee even though it was black. He was silent for a minute. Then he put the spoon down and looked straight into his brother's eyes. "You can't go around punishing yourself because Father's killer got away with it."

"I'm not punishing myself," Brian said. "I'm punishing the other guys."

"What have you built for yourself?" Bill asked. "You lost your wife. You've no family, nothing to work for."

"I'm not in the building business," Brian said. "I tear things down. You ran away; maybe that's right for you. But I'm staying here and fighting back."

"That won't bring Father back," Bill said.

Brian signaled a waiter and pointed at his empty water glass. "No, you're probably right about that." The waiter filled the glass from a silver pitcher, and Brian drank half of it. "But I can put other killers away. That may not be as good as it could be, but it's the best I can do. I've caught fifteen of them so far. What have you done?"

"You make me feel like I failed Father by letting you go like this. There's more to life than catching killers."

"You were at the university when Father was killed," Brian said. "That's where he wanted you to be. He worked hard to get you there. You could have come back after graduation, but you stayed. You've got the good business, the good wife, the kids. No one's blaming you for doing well. But you can't stop me from doing what I have to do."

Bill signaled for the check. He tossed his American Express card on the table. Brian snatched the card and laid five twenties on the check.

"You know, I did steal five of your Yankee cards," Brian said. "Father, he left the safe open one night."

"I figured it was you." Bill laughed. Brian started to get up, but Bill put a hand on his arm. "There's one other thing. Who's going to carry on the family name if you don't get married and have sons? You're forcing my girls to marry men who will let them keep their own names, and guys like that aren't easy to find in Indiana."

* * *

When Dr. Don Dooley finished putting the supper dishes in the dishwasher, he joined his wife Sharon in the study where she was lighting the fire. He poured the chablis and they settled down at opposing desks to make their daily journal entries.

They wrote silently through the first glass. Then as Don poured the second glass, Sharon asked, "Have you heard from that editor who was so excited about your book?"

"Not yet," Don said, and Sharon made a note of it in her journal. He watched her writing and said, "Having my books rejected hasn't been a totally negative experience for me. I've learned something important from my tribulations."

Sharon put down her pen. "What would that be, dear?"

"How to deal with rejection." Don paced behind Sharon's desk, staring at the back of her neck. She had been a ballet dancer years ago and her distinguishing features were still her swan neck and over-muscled legs. "I was having problems with it until I realized that it's not my fault my books keep getting rejected. It's their fault."

"You always said we had to be responsible for our own lives," Sharon pointed out.

"That's why I blamed myself for my failures." Don touched her neck, feeling the muscles tighten. "Then I had my breakthrough."

Sharon shifted in her chair, but he kept his hand on her neck. "Do you want to share it with me?" She leaned forward for her glass, and he started pacing again.

"I realized what was true for life wasn't necessarily true for publishing. I couldn't be responsible for my books being rejected because if it were up to me, they would have been published. It wasn't me, so it had to be them. It's their fault."

Sharon finished her wine, got the bottle, and filled her glass again. "I understand how you could feel that way."

Don leaned against the stone fireplace watching her throat as she swallowed. "You can't imagine how free I felt. No more guilt, no more agonizing self-recriminations. Now I can concentrate on what needs to be done."

"And what might that be, dear?"

"Behavior modification." Don refilled her wine glass again. "I will modify their behavior until they publish my books. This won't be easy, but I have a plan and sooner or later my plan shall succeed. It has to. It's fool-proof."

"Aren't you going to share it with me?"

"You'll have to wait until I succeed," Don said, circling behind her. She turned in her chair to follow him, and he watched the long muscles of her neck twist. "If I told you now, it would ruin the suspense."

As Don put his hand back on her neck, Sharon rose, went to the bar, and opened another bottle of chablis. "Don't you think it would be a good idea to start work on your next book?"

Don lay down on a leather couch. "Perhaps I'll do a mystery about a psychiatrist who kills his patients because their problems are driving him mad."

"We've had killer psychiatrists before."

"We have?"

"Several times, and there was that movie, I believe."

"That's the book world for you," Don said. "An industry that feeds on new ideas is doomed to go hungry."

"I've had a thought."

"Would you like to share it with us?"

"Why not something a little different?" Sharon suggested. "The wife of a psychiatrist. She's the killer."

"But what is her motive?"

"She's sick and tired of her husband's patients taking up their lives."

"I see. I didn't realize you felt that way."

"It's only an idea for a book."

"Yes, what isn't?" He stared at the photo of swans on the wall opposite the couch. He had taken that photo himself, although many people assumed it was the work of a professional photographer. "I have to write, you know. I can't stop until I succeed."

"But you're already a very successful psychiatrist." Sharon rubbed her neck, where her muscles were knotting.

"That's not me. That's my patients. It's their problems. My

writing is the only thing that's mine. That's why I have to succeed as a writer. Rejection means I'm a failure."

"Only if you take it that way."

"No, it has nothing to do with ego. It's a matter of professional credibility. I can't have the competition saying, 'If old Dooley is so smart, why can't he even get a stupid mystery published?' It would ruin me."

He jumped off the couch. Sharon grabbed the empty chablis bottle by the neck. Don crossed to his typing table, put in a piece of paper and started typing, hitting the keys hard. Sharon rubbed her neck.

"You'll make it work," she said, although Don no longer heard her. "I can feel it."

On only two glasses of wine, Anne had written fifteen pages, background chapters about the two slain editors.

It was amazing how easy it was to write, how quickly it came to her, in what concentrated and fluid form. Whereas when she'd first tried to become a writer six years ago, it was agonizing. Slow and blocked and in constant need of editing that she simply could not bear to do.

What made this book so easy to write? Was it her celibacy or her contract? Didn't matter. Either way, she was going to write a great crime story and it was going to sell.

There was only one conceivable problem: What if Brian Skiles didn't catch the killer?

Two problems: What if Brian Skiles caught him too late?

Anne poured herself a third glass of wine and stared out the window at the dark apartments across the street. Was there, she wondered, someone staring back?"

Chapter 27

ANNE GOT TO THE office early the next morning and looked over what she had written the previous night. The stuff was good, didn't need much revising.

But there was a residue in her mouth, not of wine but of fear. What if the killer wasn't stalking her? What if he was? And Brian Skiles, a guy who fell off chairs, a guy in trouble with his boss, and his ex-wife.

What good would Brian be to her? He was a cop, but this cop was a man. Could he rise above it? Or when the killer pounced, would he fall off some other kind of chair?

When Brian came into the office at 9:30, Anne glared at him in response to his greeting. Good thing I'm not really working for her, he thought sourly.

What was he working for, he wondered, and would he ever get it?

The office heater was back on now, too hot. He hung up his coat and jacket and put his gun in the desk drawer without the screws. He sat down and began to skim manuscripts.

Half an hour later, Brian looked up and said, "I didn't realize so many books could be so bad."

Anne was startled at first. She had slipped into that private, shut-out world that books and editing always let her enter. She looked over at Brian and thought, There's a man of the world and welcome to it.

"No one ever does," she said, "until you read fifty of them. Then the conclusion is inescapable."

"Why can't they tell how bad their books are before they send them in to you?"

"Why do fat men whistle at beautiful women? People write mystery novels to prove how clever they are. Then we reject them, proving that they're not so clever after all. No wonder they want to kill us." It was cold in the room, she thought, not when it was a room of books but when it was a room in the world, which it hadn't been until Brian Skiles had entered, bringing his murders with him like unwanted in-laws.

Brian shook his head, slapping his hand on a pile of manuscripts. "Sounds like a crazy way to make a living."

"And being a cop is the sign of a well-adjusted man," Anne said with a venom that both surprised and didn't surprise Brian.

Anne and Brian were both so busy wondering why the other one was being a jerk that they didn't notice the office door open and Brandon Everall slip inside.

"The problem with men," Anne continued, "is that once you get to know them, you forget what it was that made you want to know them in the first place." She glared across her desk at Brian.

Brian glared back across his desk. "The problem with women is they're always finding problems with men."

Brandon clasped his hands together. "Glad to see the two of you not getting along. Keep up the good work."

Brian looked at Brandon who had, somehow, grown tanner overnight. Jauntier too, his hair more silver, his teeth longer and whiter, his smirk more in need of a stiff right cross.

Anne sighed, thinking even men of immense wealth and sophistication were still men. Although if you had to have a man around, the least he could do was wear hand-made suits, have silvery hair, and be completely insincere. Insincerity was something you could trust in a man.

Brandon waved happily and left the office.

"What's the matter with that guy?" Brian asked.

"Nothing that's not the matter with you too," Anne said. "He wants to have everything his way."

"The man's got a problem," Brian insisted. "Why does he keep thinking there's something going on between us?"

"Because if he were you, there would be."

"Then I'm glad he's not me."

"So am I."

This was ridiculous, Brian thought, arguing about nothing with someone who meant nothing to him. "We have nothing in common," he said.

The nerve of this cop, Anne thought, thinking she had nothing in common with him when the truth was that he had nothing in common with her. "We're completely different," she said. "I want to be witty and glamorous, and you want to shoot someone."

"Let's get to work," Brian said.

Twenty minutes later, the door opened and a woman who looked like she was trying to look like Faye Dunaway walked in. She was tall, icy, and blonde. She wore black sunglasses and a full-length mink coat. She carried a large leather bag.

She glanced at Anne, dismissed her and walked over to Brian's desk, peering down at him from behind impenetrable sunglasses. "Here's your next best-seller," she said, opening the leather bag with the golden clasp.

"Great delivery service," Brian said. "How do you manage to ride a messenger bike in that fur?"

She ignored his remark and handed him a manuscript packed inside a box from Bloomingdale's. He glanced at the typed label on the top of the box. It read: *The Case of the Missing ________,* a mystery novel by Jillian Fissure.

"I am Jillian Fissure," she said, "the author."

"Why didn't you simply mail it in?" he asked.

"The post office is so passé, don't you agree?"

"Is this your first book?"

"My first really important book," Jillian said. "What do people want from life?" She ran her hands along the mink lapels of her coat. A diamond flashed on her left hand; an emerald shone on her right. "A few laughs and a carload of money. But there has to be something more, something that makes it all worthwhile. What makes life worth the effort is feeling superior to other people. Look at them. They're depressing. Only by feeling better than them can you escape their depression."

"Writing a book makes you feel better?" Brian asked.

"No, writing a book makes me feel tired," Jillian said. "But getting my book published will make me feel superior to everyone who hasn't had a book published, and that's most people. I'm already better looking than practically everyone, and my husband has more money. I have the latest clothes and the right car, and I go on all the important vacations. Now I want a book with my name on it, and you're going to give it to me."

"What makes you think I'm going to do that?" Brian asked.

"Because you're not important enough to say no to me."

Brian looked over Jillian's shoulder and saw Anne laughing silently, enjoying his predicament. "What have you been doing for a living while waiting to become a famous writer?" he asked.

"Oh, dinner, the vital parties," Jillian said. "Society, you know."

"Then you don't have a job?"

"I don't understand the question. My husband has a job."

"What does he do?"

Jillian smiled at him the way the president of a Fortune 100 company will smile at a cab driver who has just asked him for financial advice. "He makes money," she said. "I spend it. We have one of those fifty-fifty relationships."

"There is one chance," Brian said. "For your book. Our new program to publish undiscovered writers whose books have been rejected by other publishers."

"I do not get rejected," Jillian said. "Ever. However, I did show my book to some other publishers, and they did not come up with an acceptable offer. That's why I decided to help your company by letting you publish it."

"Fine. Then if you'll leave your book, we'll read it and see if it's right for us," Brian said.

"Is that necessary? Can't you simply take my word?"

"It's our standard procedure for making decisions on books. First, we read them."

"Bureaucracy," Jillian sighed. She placed the manuscript in the Bloomingdale's box on the desk and stood up, angling herself toward him like a fashion model. "There is one more thing," she said. "When people look at a writer like me, they think I'm all brain. They don't realize that I have a great body too."

Jillian ran her hands up the mink and pulled back the coat. She was naked underneath.

Brian stared at Jillian's high breasts, flat stomach, and flared hips. When she closed the coat again, a perfect mental image of her body remained.

"If you were my editor, we'd have to work closely together," Jillian said. "Very closely."

"There's only one problem," Brian said. "I'm not the editor here. She is."

Jillian looked annoyed. She pivoted and looked at Anne. Then she shrugged and pulled back her coat again. "And what does someone like you think of something like this?"

"Very nice," Anne said. "Did you want to write the book or simply pose for the front cover?"

Jillian moved to the door. "I was born to be mysterious," she said. "When you think of foggy nights, tragic love affairs, and smoking guns, think of me." She opened the door and spun through it. Anne clapped her hands twice. Then she and Brian laughed together for the first time.

"What do you think of our Jillian Fissure?" Brian asked.

"She's a knockout," Anne said. "I hate her, I suppose. What do you think of her? And more important, how often?"

"She's not a likely killer," Brian said. "When the beautiful people murder, they kill their own."

"But there is that something in her eyes," Anne said. "She's capable of anything."

Brian slipped Jillian's manuscript into a large envelope. "Why are so many writers coming in now?"

"It's the season," Anne said. "End of winter. They've been holed up inside for months, writing their little fingers off. Now they want to inflict the result on the world."

Brian picked up the envelope and moved to the door. "I want to get these prints down to the lab. You're not going to work late, are you?"

"I have to go to a book party," Anne said. "Why don't you meet me there? You can see how the published writers make the unpublished ones look normal."

As Rep Gates unlocked the storeroom in the back of Mac's Place, he looked at the *Playboy* centerfolds pinned to the wall behind the cartons of boozc.

Next time, I'll pin Melanie to the wall, he thought. Last night, he'd had her just about every other way. She had an imagination, good inspiration for a writer.

Rep opened up the alley door. The beer truck backed up to the door, and the delivery man swung out of the cab. He grabbed the dolly and piled cartons of beer onto it.

"So you can take care of me?" Rep asked.

The delivery man nodded and wheeled the dolly into the storeroom. "Shut the door," he said. Rep unloaded the cartons of beer, while he wrote up a sales slip. When Rep bent down to lift up the last carton of beer, the delivery man put his boot across the top.

He squatted down, opened both flaps, and took out a stack of beer posters. Underneath the posters were a dozen handguns.

"See something that does it for you?" he asked.

Chapter 28

Jillian Fissure felt her muscles go, Ahhh. She smiled at Kelly Shea, who was lying on the next massage couch with a look on her face that said her muscles were going, Ahhh, too.

"Of course, they hung Jen's cute little paintings in their museum," Jillian said. "Her father donated a million dollars to the new wing."

"They would hang Jen there if she asked," Kelly agreed. "And they should."

Kelly closed her eyes and sighed in dreamy pleasure, as the Japanese Shiatsuizer, who never spoke but also never stopped working over the bodies of her wealthy clients, applied magical pressure with her tiny-headed vibrator to just the right spots on Kelly's body.

It was called Acuvibe, combining the ancient wisdom of Chinese acupuncture with the most advanced Western electronics for the Club's rich clients, who wanted any relief they could get but did not want to be stuck with needles in the process. Providing the latest in personal service was what the Club was all about.

Taking advantage of whatever she could was what Jillian Fissure was all about. So she shut her own eyes as her own personal Japanese Shiatsuizer applied the magical touches that made Jillian's body feel that everything would work out, a feeling that Jillian's mind did not always agree with. Jillian's mind couldn't shake free of the editors who were constantly thwarting her efforts to publish her novels. Why couldn't editors be more like personal Japanese Shiatsuizers, more service-oriented?

Jillian looked at Kelly, who was now securely half asleep, comforted by the knowledge that she was rich, fat-free, and well-attended. And also that she played viola well enough to be asked to join a discreet quartet that performed at select affairs.

Jillian felt her back muscles tense at the thought of Kelly's success. But the Japanese Shiatsuizer felt it also and was right there with her acu-vibrator to counter the tension. Ahh, service, Jillian thought, it was what life was all about.

We spend our lives having our edges smoothed, hiring people to keep the details polished. We married the right men, lived in the right places, looked right at all significant times. But there was always something new that could turn all your rights to wrong. Some new criteria by which all are judged, and only the right few shall pass.

Jillian had always passed. She had the looks, the money, the passage into the right circles. But now everyone had that. Too many people had caught up with her. One had to do something to rise above the pack.

In desperation, people had turned to talent as the latest trend. Accomplishment was the new status symbol. Art, music, dance, writing. It was no longer enough to be the best. You now had to do something too.

Because Jillian's gift was to discover trends before they were certified by the *New York Times* she had started early. She chose writing as her field of accomplishment because art was too risky (critics were so judgmental) and music required actual talent. But books were written by people of no standing whatsoever.

If they could write, she could. And the act of writing, she quickly found out, felt so good when you had taken just the right amount of the very best diet pills. So Jillian had taken her pills religiously and written regularly, feeling intensely sure of accomplishment and the rewards it would bring.

Jillian Fissure, the mysterious mystery writer. So beautiful, so rich, so talented. Jillian, we were at the Trumps the other night, and we saw all your books on their shelf. Jillian, how do you do it?

She did it by doing everything right. And yet, it all went wrong.

Jillian wrote her first novel in three months, a mystery. Mysteries were easy to write because you knew they had a beginning and an end, which meant you could figure out where you were going. Books about life weren't nearly so clear.

But no one bought her first book. So Jillian increased her dosage of diet pills and wrote her second mystery in two months. It was also rejected, more times than she cared to think about. What she couldn't stop thinking about was that her time was running out.

As the trend toward accomplishment as status symbol became established and was identified by the V's (the *Village Voice* first, and then *Vanity Fair*), Jillian knew her opportunity for success was tightening around her like a choker of imitation pearls.

Worse, people were whispering that she wrote but not well. That she wanted to get published but could not. The gossip gave her a public air of desperation, to which there was no antidote but success. She had to prove them wrong and fast, before her failure proved them right. There was nothing sadder in society than a ruined person who tries for a trend and misses.

Jillian had finished her last mystery in three weeks, working through the amphetamine nights, and she would have this one published. There was simply no other choice left.

Suddenly, Kelly sat up, startling Jillian from her reverie. As Kelly's Japanese Shiatsuizer lightly placed a silk robe around her bare shoulders, Jillian's pushed the acu-vibrator into a higher gear.

"I must positively flee," Kelly announced. "I have a rehearsal in five minutes. We've promised to play at the Historical Society's benefit. You are coming, aren't you?"

"Probably," Jillian said, looking at Kelly's hands and wondering why she hadn't kept up with her own childhood piano lessons. Music was so much simpler than writing. You didn't have to think, and everyone always said how nicely you played. No one ever rejected you.

Kelly opened her robe and studied her body in the wall of mirrors. "God, I remember when it was enough just to be gorgeous and rich. Now you have to be good at something too. Thank God, I have my music. I don't know what I would do if I was just married to your common millionaire."

Chapter 29

WHEN BRIAN ENTERED the health club, a perky young woman in shorts and a T-shirt that said I'M FIT FOR YOU asked him for his membership card. He showed her his police badge instead and asked to see Cathy McDougald.

"Cathy's helping people right now," the woman said. "They're doing aerobics, so they can't stop. She didn't do anything wrong, did she?"

"Felony fitness," Brian said.

"What's that? I mean, looking good isn't a crime, is it?"

"How about I wait for her in the lounge?"

"Sure, it's on your left past the weight room."

The weight room had glass walls so people who weren't working out could watch the people who were. Inside the room, a dozen very large men with very few clothes on were going through two-hour workouts, inching up their muscles, cutting down their fat.

Brian felt uncomfortable and remembered the sit-ups and jogging he had put on his schedule right before he lost the schedule. They build muscles, he thought, the way medieval kings built walls around their castles—the more walls they added, the safer they thought they were. Until some smart little guy figured out a way to blow their walls down.

Brian went into the lounge, where a muscular young man was chatting with two middle-aged women in expensive sweatsuits. They drank mineral water and glanced up at a screen where a videotape was playing, Cathy leading a workout. She looked fantastic in her high-cut, low-cut leotard and shiny tights.

Then Cathy walked into the room looking even better than she did on the screen. "Did you come to work out, Brian?" she asked. "Or have you been following me?"

"Anne Baker said you went to see her," Brian said.

"She's sweet," Cathy said. "Tall too. But not the woman for you. She's even more wrong for you than I was."

"You're looking good, Cathy."

"I've got things going my way. My classes are too popular, and I'll get a good deal on the book. Some investors want me to start my own chain of clubs. Much nicer than this, of course. And it's all happening because I've become the complete woman."

"What does that mean, Cathy, the complete woman?"

"It's everything I've studied: aerobics, bodybuilding, tantric yoga."

The middle-aged women left the lounge, looking unhappy. The bodybuilder smiled at Cathy and followed them out, flexing his massive biceps as he passed Brian.

"My basic idea," Cathy said, "is that no woman can take complete control of her life until she has complete control of her body. That's what tantric yoga taught me. I've become so Eastern since I saw you last."

"I knew there was something different about you," Brian said.

"Look at the poor Western woman," Cathy said. "She has to learn about sexuality from the worst possible teacher: Western man. They know nothing because they've never had training. What can a woman do? Somehow she is expected to please her man and herself too. Whereas, in the East, we have studied the art of love for centuries. I feel sorry for you that we were married before I took the training. It's something everyone should experience."

"I'm sure everyone will."

"You sound bitter," Cathy said. "I must have hurt you terribly. Want a Perrier?" She took a bottle from the cooler, tossed back her head, and swallowed half.

"I've been busy," Brian said. "The work goes on. Crime never sleeps."

"It's all right if you're still angry with me," Cathy said.

"Yes, I remember how it goes. I say one thing, and you make it into something else. Then I get confused, and you win."

"You're such a cop," Cathy said. "Mr. Suspicion."

"I was a cop when you married me. If you didn't like what I was, you should have married someone who was what you wanted me to be."

"I married the man you could have been. You got stuck somewhere. But that's the past. Now we must decide our futures. I want you, Brian."

Cathy swallowed the last of the Perrier. She looked at him. He looked back at her. She put her arms around his neck and kissed him. He kissed her back. She slid into his lap and kissed him harder. He kissed her harder back.

"You have something Hank will never have," Cathy said. "That intensity, that purpose. Maybe you don't have his ambition or success, but I can afford to let that go now. You bring to love a feeling that it's really important. That's what I need. You're my lover for life."

She kissed him again. This time he didn't kiss her back. She stood up and walked away.

"If I take you back, you'll give up Hank?" Brian asked.

Cathy shrugged. "The man's going to be important, but he is a pompous fool."

"And if I don't take you back?"

She turned half way and looked at him. He stared at her sleek profile. "Then I'll marry Hank and ruin your career," she said. "No more cops and robbers."

"You think you can do that?"

"Brian, of course I can."

"Why would you want to ruin my career, Cathy?"

"I'm a spiteful person, Brian. It's not something I'm really proud of. But I've learned to accept that in myself."

"And you'd marry Hank even though you don't love him?"

"Hank is not the kind of man you love. He is the kind of man you can strike a good bargain with. So what's it going to be, Brian?"

"You trying to blackmail me, Cathy?"

"If I can't have one thing I want, then I intend to have something else. Why should I be left with nothing?"

He stood up. She smiled and opened her arms. "Sorry, Cathy, but it would never work out."

Her hands closed into fists, and she glared at him. "You might as well hand in your badge right now. You're through as a cop."

"I don't think so."

"You don't think at all," Cathy said. "I'm going to tell Hank right now."

"I doubt it," Brian said.

"What's going to stop me?" Cathy raised her fists. "You're not tough enough."

Brian patted his pocket. "I've got our conversation on tape." He took out the small tape recorder.

"You bastard."

"I was married to you for three years, Cathy. I guess I learned something in all that time." He headed for the door.

"Sooner or later, Brian, I'm going to get you," Cathy said. "I'm a lot meaner than you are."

Chapter 30

BRIAN RODE UP to the penthouse in an elevator with three skinny people in black, two of them women.

"Did you hear the police are about to make an arrest in the book murders?" said the blonde with the blue streak in her hair.

"Of course, it will be the wrong one," the man said. He had silver highlights in black hair.

"I heard a good one today," said the woman with green points on her red bangs. "How many kidnappers does it take to ransom an editor?"

"Who'd pay the ransom?" the man asked.

"No," red-green insisted. "The answer is two. One to write the note and one to proofread it for spelling mistakes."

"There's one good thing you can say about editors," blonde-blue said. "At least they're not writers." All three of them glanced back at Brian, wondering whether he was a writer, although he looked too normal to be one.

The elevator opened on the penthouse. The trio in black spotted the bar and veered toward it. Brian spotted Anne across the crowded room. She met him under the wall of Andy Warhols. "I didn't think you'd actually come," she said. "You do have nerve."

"I'm used to going where I'm not necessarily wanted," Brian said. A waiter offered them champagne from a tray. Anne plucked off two glasses.

"Have a drink," she said.

"Not now." He scanned the dozens of people at the party.

Anne downed one glass and set it in the pot of a large cactus. She sipped from the second. "If you don't drink, this won't make any sense to you."

"I'll fake it," Brian said. "Are all these people writers and editors?"

"Some." Anne leaned close and whispered, "But the good-looking ones are the money people. They like to attend book parties because it makes them feel good to know they could buy and sell everyone in the room. Hell, they could rent everyone in the room. It reminds them how smart it was of them not to become intellectual."

"I'll act suitably impressed," Brian said.

"Jealousy is the emotion to shoot for." Anne finished her second champagne and balanced the empty on top of the first glass. "Let's drift," she said.

Anne took Brian's arm and led him about the party. In the library a dozen people were competing to see who could create the tallest stack of books on the floor. A man and a woman came up behind them.

"Did you hear the Publishers' Association is offering a reward for catching the book killer?" the woman asked Anne.

"Yes, but the Writers' Guild is offering a medal," the man said.

"Brian, I don't think you've met Margie Marx," Anne said. "She works in our sales department. And this is the famous essayist, Vincent Chettingham, who is also, in his more frivolous moments, the mystery writer Todd Blanks. Brian is my new assistant editor."

"I thought I'd seen you around the office," Margie said.

"If you do mysteries, call me Todd," the man said. "Can you edit?"

"Only when I have to," Brian said.

"I'm going to give you some advice," Todd said. "Whatever you do while working for Ms. Baker, remember one thing: don't ever, ever touch one of my books. Not a word, not a mark of punctuation. Then we'll get along fine. Or at least I shall, and that's what counts."

"Your books never need editing," Anne said. "That's why they're such a pleasure to deal with."

"They make you money, my sweet," Todd said. "That's why

they never need editing. I'm fully aware that if my sales should slip, you would suddenly find many things that could be improved in my books."

"But your sales have never slipped," Margie said.

"And they won't, but do you know why?" Todd asked.

"Good editing," Brian said.

"Hardly," Todd said. "It's because I chose a pen name that begins with one of the letters B, F, or M. Best-selling letters all. In serious literature, it's a totally different story, of course. C-names do well there, as do J-names and R-names. My real name happens to be Zabriskie, but I would have been a failure in the Z's. Z-names are typically shelved down by people's ankles, and no one reads that low. You two go circulate before I scare you out of the business and Anne never forgives me for it."

Anne and Brian approached the buffet table, where a very fat man and a very skinny woman were examining the food. "He's a cookbook writer," Anne said. "She writes diet books."

"It's a matter of teamwork," the fat man said. "I feed them until they feel guilty enough to buy your diet books."

"Eventually, they get so tired of my diets," the woman said, "that they buy your cookbooks. It's a delicious cycle."

"I'm going to get a drink. You want one?" Anne asked.

"No, I'll circulate," Brian said. "I'd like to see if I'm any good at this."

Anne crossed the room to the bar and asked for a double martini. One of the smaller literary agents, whose name she kept confusing with other small literary agents she always forgot, zeroed in on her. Anne took a long drink.

"I've got a book for your eyes only," the agent said in a low voice. "I wouldn't sell it to anyone else."

"That bad, is it?"

"Love your cynical bits, Anne darling," the agent said. "Don't ever lose them. No, the truth is Jessica Brody was all set to buy this book before she was killed, the poor dear. The last thing she said to me was, 'If anything should happen to me, make sure Anne Baker gets this book.' I'm going to sell it to you as a last request kind of thing."

"I'm touched."

"I'll messenger it over in the morning."

Meanwhile, Brian strolled through the penthouse, watching the party people and listening to wisps of conversation. He felt a hand run up his arm. He turned and was a breath away from Claire Deluthe, Everall's romance editor.

She squeezed his bicep. "You've worked for our little Annie for what, a week now?"

"About."

"Then you must come to work for me."

"Why?"

"I take away all her boyfriends," Claire said. "It's a little something we have between us."

"I'm not her boyfriend," Brian said.

"Why else would she hire you?"

"To help her edit books."

"Don't be silly," Claire said. "Books aren't edited. They're sold. You come to work for me, darling, but be sure to steal one of her top-selling authors and bring her with you."

Anne and her double martini joined them. "There's something different about your dress tonight, Claire," she said.

Claire looked warily at Anne. "What?"

"It's still on," Anne said.

"Your new assistant, if that's what he really is, has been begging me for a job," Claire said. "Really, Anne dearest, you must learn to treat people better than they've treated you."

Anne and Brian stepped out onto the balcony and looked up at the starry night.

"Are there really that many stars?" Anne asked, leaning against the railing. "Or am I seeing double?"

"Look what I see." Brian pointed over to a smaller balcony outside one of the penthouse bedrooms.

A couple stood in intimate conversation: Brandon Everall and Jillian Fissure.

"We might publish your book, Jillian, under the right conditions," Brandon said, filling her glass with champagne and looking down her dress.

"I love books, you know," Jillian said, leaning into him so he could get a better view. "Especially, the older, distinguished kind. They feel so lovely covered in leather. Sometimes, I want to take one to bed with me, curl up under the covers and stay all night, reading, reading, reading until I can't see straight."

Brandon put down the champagne bottle, and Jillian came into his arms. They kissed and headed into the bedroom.

"Now there's a writer who doesn't need an agent," Anne said.

"You wait here," Brian said. "I'm going over and take a look."

"You voyeur."

"Police business."

"Right. Then I'm going with you. I want to see this for myself."

Brian shrugged. It was an easy jump from one balcony to the next. He pulled himself up on the ledge and stepped across. Anne swung onto the ledge, stepped over unsteadily and whispered, "Thank God I'm drunk."

They edged over to the bedroom door and looked through the glass. Brandon sat on the edge of a bed while Jillian did a literary striptease for him.

"Here's the stuff," Jillian said, unhooking her dress, "that dreams are made of." The dress fell to the floor. Jillian was naked underneath.

Brandon lifted his glass. "Here's looking at you, kid."

Chapter 31

THE TALL BLONDE in the trenchcoat felt mysterious as she walked down thc cmpty corridor. No fear, no anger, not even excitement.

Only a delicious taste of mystery, a sensation that Bogie was watching over her shoulder. Her fingers tightened on the revolver in her trenchcoat.

The only thing missing was fog, she thought. But then you couldn't expect the corridors of a major publishing house to be shrouded in fog. Still it would have been the perfect finishing touch.

The blonde paused outside the door marked Mystery Division. She had an important decision to make. Should she pull the gun first and then go in? Or go in first and draw the gun once she was inside?

Drawing the gun first was the sensible thing to do. But going in empty-handed so the Bitch could wonder what she was doing in the office at such a late hour when no one else was supposed to be there—that was more mysterious.

She opened the door and stepped inside. The Bitch looked up from her desk, where she was editing a manuscript. "You?" she said. "What are you doing here?"

That was the perfect mysterious question, the blonde decided as she pulled the revolver from the trenchcoat and pointed it at her head.

Behind her desk, the Bitch froze, and the blonde almost shot her before she remembered the most important thing of all, the touch that would bring the mysterious feeling to its climax.

"You bitch," she said. Then she shot her.

"Cab?" the doorman asked, swinging the front door open wide.

"Broomstick," Anne said. She took a last swig from the champagne bottle and handed it to the doorman. "I'm flying tonight."

Brian caught up to her on the sidewalk. "I'm taking you home," he said.

"I've been there," Anne said. "Take me to Paris instead." She whirled about, thinking of Loretta Young, and fell into his arms.

"This way to Paris." Brian carried her down the street to his car. She giggled, waving at a couple walking their dog. He leaned her against the car, got the door open and put her inside. He went around, got behind the wheel and started the engine. She put her hand over his.

"It's amazing, aren't we?" Anne asked. "We've worked together all this time, you and I, and we haven't fallen in love. Not once."

"Amazing."

"And refreshing," Anne pointed out. "If we were most people, we'd not only have fallen in love by now but out of it again."

"Split up and made up at least twice," Brian added.

"I'd have found out all the little things about you that would drive me crazy," Anne said. "Which wrong way you squeeze the toothpaste."

"Where you throw your dirty clothes."

"What you're like when you're grumpy."

"None of which we know," Brian said, "since we haven't fallen in love."

"Then why are we sitting here in the cold?" Anne asked. "Aren't you ever going to drive me home?"

Brian pulled the car into traffic. They drove in silence for two blocks. Then Anne said, "I'm not looking for the perfect man, you know. I'd settle for a B-plus."

The blonde in the trenchcoat shut the door marked Mystery Division behind her. She didn't feel so mysterious now. She felt like getting the hell out of there.

She knew the side way out. Down the back stairs and then the single dangerous moment: three quick steps across the side corridor that opened onto the lobby, where the security guard sat.

She stood at the bottom of the back stairs trying to get her breathing down into her stomach. When she felt reasonably sure she wasn't going to hyperventilate, she took the first of those three quick steps.

Only the security guard wasn't sitting behind his desk in the lobby. He was halfway down the corridor coming toward her. Could he have heard her breathing from that far away?

"Lady, stop right there," the security guard shouted.

She saw him reach for the gun at his hip and realized that she still held the revolver in her hand. She lifted it and fired at him.

He fell to the floor—or dived there. She didn't care which because now she had taken the second and third quick steps. She ran down the short stairs, pushed open the side door, and rushed across the sidewalk to the red Triumph.

As she started the car and spun the leather-covered wheel, she felt mysterious again. The Bitch dead, the guard down, and the beautiful blonde disappears into the night. The stuff of fiction, she thought. She laughed gaily and hit the accelerator.

In the building behind her, the security guard sat up on the floor, his right arm numb from where the bullet had gone in and out. But his left arm was still good, and he was lefthanded anyway. He pulled the walkie-talkie off his belt and called for help.

In Brian's car, Anne had cranked down the window and put her face into the cold wind as Brian drove, not too fast and not too slow through light traffic. "Think of all the pain we've spared each other," she said, "by not falling in love. It's a many-splendored thing, not falling in love."

"It's the best thing I've never done," Brian said.

They were silent for an awkward block. Then Anne switched on Brian's police radio. "What's this?"

"Don't, it's a police. . ."

". . . an 815 in progress," the police dispatcher said.

"What's an 815?" Anne asked.

"Shooting with a suspect in flight," Brian said.

"Suspect last seen leaving One Park Avenue in a red sports car," the dispatcher said. "Proceeding toward lower Manhattan."

"One Park?" Anne said. "That's where Vargas House is."

"What's Vargas House?" Brian asked as he swung the car around the corner, picking up speed.

"A publisher," Anne said. "Maybe they've killed another editor."

"Suspect is a Caucasian, female," the dispatcher said. "Tall, blonde hair, wearing a trenchcoat. Suspect considered armed and dangerous."

"Sounds like Jillian Fissure," Brian said. "Maybe she left the party before we did. But she was supposed to kill you."

"Sorry to disappoint," Anne said.

Brian headed the car downtown. "Murder should never be left to amateurs."

Anne was about to retaliate when they were passed by a red Triumph racing downtown. A blonde women was at the wheel with her trenchcoat collar pulled up around her neck. How wonderfully mysterious she looks, Anne thought.

Brian picked up speed and followed the Triumph through the deserted streets as sirens closed behind them.

"God, I love a good chase," Anne shouted. "Faster. Catch her. Pass her on the right."

"I'm not trying to win this race," Brian said. "I only have to come in second."

The sirens were louder now and Brian could see two police cars behind him with lights flashing. He rolled down the window and slapped a magnetic light bubble on the roof.

"Can I work the siren?" Anne asked.

Ahead of them, the Triumph braked, swerving to the right, to the left. Two police cars blocked the road. The Triumph twisted between parked cars and went up on the sidewalk. A third police car pulled up against the sidewalk at the corner to block that escape.

A few yards from the corner was a subway entrance. The Triumph went straight for it, slowed at the top, then plunged down the steps. Brian stopped by the subway entrance as the other cars came up behind him. Brian jumped out and ran for the stairs.

She'd seen this in a movie, the blonde thought as her Triumph rolled down the steps of the subway station. That French thing. The Triumph was picking up too much speed, but she wasn't sure if you should hit the brakes when you were driving down steep stairs.

Then she remembered. It wasn't a car they'd used to go down in the subway. It was a motorcycle. Would that make any difference? The Triumph hit the side wall and bounced against the middle railing. Suddenly the stairs were too steep. She hit the brakes, and the Triumph tipped end over end three times before it landed at the bottom of the stairs, spinning slowly on its roof.

Down in the subway station, the rescue crew was cutting through the wreckage. The cops up on the sidewalk crowded around Captain Stark, who had arrived shortly after the ambulance.

Anne and Brian stood off to the side, staring down the steps. She didn't look so drunk now. She looked, instead, like one of those reporters who showed up at the scene of a murder, trying hard to get a glimpse of the corpse although it would mean nothing for their stories.

"They're coming up," Anne whispered.

The medics climbed slowly from the station, the stretcher's wheels bumping up each step. The bumps weren't going to bother the stretcher's passenger though; this was her last ride.

Captain Stark stopped them. He pulled the sheet back, looked at the blonde with the broken neck and said, "We've got our book killer now. Third time is a charm."

Brian pulled Anne back toward his car. "That's not Jillian Fissure," he said.

"That's Cynthia Vargas," Anne said. "She's married to Karl Vargas. Well, she was."

They got into the car. Brian let the ambulance pass, then backed away from the curb and headed uptown. "Who's Karl Vargas?" he asked.

"President and publisher of Vargas House," Anne said. "I don't understand how Cynthia can be the killer. She's not even one of our suspects."

"It doesn't make sense," Brian said as he tried to make sense of it all.

"Unless she's right and you're wrong."

Chapter 32

BRIAN FOUND CAPTAIN STARK working in his office. "That's all right," Stark said. "I'm not too big to accept an abject apology."

"So you're going to pin all three murders on Cynthia Vargas?" Brian asked.

"Why not? She killed all three women. At least she did until someone proves she didn't."

"What have you got on her?"

Stark laughed. He put his feet up on his desk and cupped his hands behind his head. "Last night's killing, for one."

"What about the first two murders?" Brian asked. "Anything that ties Cynthia to them?"

"They fit the same pattern," Stark said. "There's never a sign of a break-in because she already has a key."

"Where does she get the key?"

"From her husband," Stark said. "He's the publisher at Vargas House. Any other questions?" Stark seemed to be enjoying himself, which men who thought they had all the answers often did.

"Plenty," Brian said. "Where did Cynthia get keys to the other two offices?"

"Simple. Her husband had worked at both places before starting his own company. He probably kept the keys, and she took them from him."

"Have you checked with the husband to see if his own key is missing?"

"She could have taken his key, had a copy made and returned it before he knew it was gone."

"Why would she kill the first two women?"

"The husband says his wife thought he had affairs with both of them. She was insanely jealous."

"Now you're taking second-hand confessions?"

"I'm taking evidence," Stark said. "And it all points to Cynthia Vargas being the book killer."

"She used a twenty-two last night," Brian said. "The first two victims were killed with a thirty-eight."

"There's no law that says a killer can't have more than one gun. It's a free country."

"And what about the rejection note?" Brian asked. "Cynthia didn't leave one with the victim last night."

"So she got tired of that gag," Stark said. "I was tired of it too. I told you before that those rejection notes had nothing to do with solving the case."

Brian paced in front of Stark's desk. "It doesn't add up. A jealous wife might kill the woman who stole her husband. But she wouldn't kill three women. If he was playing around that much, she'd be used to it. She'd give up."

"That's your theory anyway," Stark said, watching Brian and knowing that all his pacing, all his efforts weren't going to do him any good—with solving the case or keeping his job. "My theory is I've caught the killer and it solves all three cases. As in case closed. That's why my theory is so much better than yours."

Brian stopped pacing. "What if your theory is wrong and someone else gets killed?"

Stark grinned. "Life, in general, is tough and then you die. Now get out of here and stay out. This case is closed."

"No, it's not," Brian said. "There's a killer loose out there, and I'm going to catch him."

"Then you catch yours, because I've caught mine."

Chapter 33

LOGIC TOLD ANNE that she had felt worse sometime before in her life. The odds said that she must have had a worse hangover before. But she didn't believe logic and she didn't trust luck. This was not only the worst hangover she'd ever had, it was the worst in the history of the western world. And major drunken parts of China.

She sat at her desk wondering whether she should rip up every page of the pointless book she had been writing. Or would it be more satisfying and less noisy to toss it in the fire?

Then Brian walked in the office. Now here's a tougher question, Anne thought: Rip him in half or simply toss him away?

"Looks like it's over," Brian said.

"Feels like it too," Anne said. "But I don't remember you drinking that much at the party."

"I should have gotten drunk," Brian said despondently. "Maybe then I would have hit Cynthia Vargas' car and saved her life."

"Was Cynthia the book killer?"

"The captain thinks so," Brian said. "He'll try to pin all three murders on her."

"Don't tell me," Anne said. "Let me take a wild guess about what's going on here. Detective Brian Skiles doesn't believe his captain could ever catch the right killer without the fearless help of Detective Brian Skiles. No, Brian thinks the only thing his captain could ever catch is Detective Brian Skiles' wife."

"Ex-wife," Brian corrected.

"Says you."

"It doesn't matter what you think of me or how disappointed you are or how nasty you choose to be," Brian said. "There are facts here. And Stark doesn't have them. He can't be right. I can't be wrong. It doesn't work that way."

"Don't preach to me about facts, you morbidly average detective masquerading as a tragically average human being. You're just like all my would-be mystery writers, trying to be smarter than everyone else. And that's what makes you dumber."

"You're a little tense today, aren't you, Anne?"

"I've had it with all your murder theories," Anne said. "I've had it with your alleged investigation. And most of all I've had it with you."

"Are you trying to tell me that you've had it?"

"You've had it too, buddy," Anne said. "This case is over, and you lost. Say goodnight, Gracie."

"I never wanted to write that book anyhow," Brian said.

"I never wanted to catch a killer," Anne said. "Nothing but kids playing cops and robbers with other people's lives."

"Then I guess I'll be going."

"Don't keep talking about it. Just get out of here."

Brian turned to the door. "That's what you said the first time we met."

Anne looked down at her desk, the afterglow of battle beginning to resemble her hangover. "You should have listened to me then."

She didn't look up as Brian left. She was an editor, a professional, and she had work to do. She searched her desk for some work, picked up the mail from her in-box.

Brian took three steps down the hall, turned and walked two steps back, turned and walked four away, turned and stared at the door marked Mystery Division. The hell with it, he thought. If a man can't stay, he ought to know how to leave.

He was four steps from the lobby when he heard Anne scream.

When Brian burst through the door, gun drawn, he saw Anne standing behind her desk, holding a letter, her hand shaking.

"What?" Brian asked.

"He's going to kill me!" Anne said.

Brian spun around in a crouch. No one. He slammed against the wall and edged toward the storage closet. He pushed the door open with the barrel of his gun and looked inside. No one.

"Not there," Anne said. "Here!" Brian spun around, covering the windows. Anne waved the letter at him. "It's a death note, I mean a death threat. I mean, I'm next."

Brian put his gun away. He went behind Anne's desk and looked at the letter. On a plain piece of white paper, the killer had pasted words cut out from newspapers. The words said: "Publish or perish. Purchase my book or you'll be the next to go."

"It's not signed," Anne said. "How am I supposed to know whose book to publish?"

Brian looked at the envelope lying on Anne's desk. "This is the breakthrough I've been waiting for," he said. "The envelope is addressed to both of us: Anne Baker and Brian Skiles, Editors, Everall Publishing."

"Swell, a double murder. What a perfect way to end a perfect relationship."

"The killer thinks I work here," Brian said. "That's why he's threatening both of us."

"So we told a little lie," Anne said. "People who lie together die together."

"But we've only told that lie to four writers," Brian said. "The four writers who've brought their books into the office over the past week: Don Dooley, Brigid O'Hare, Rep Gates, and Jillian Fissure. They're the only writers who think I work here. The killer has to be one of them. We're back in business."

Anne thought it over for a minute. "Call the captain and get me some police protection. Something big and blue."

"He wouldn't believe me," Brian said.

"You mean you want to catch the killer yourself so you can show the captain up," Anne said. "You're still trying to prove to your wife that you're the best man. And you're willing to risk my life to do it."

"You want a best-seller, don't you?" Brian asked. "You tell me which way will sell more books."

"You bastard. You're as bad as I am."

"Thank you."

Anne shivered once, then her eyes got steely. "All right, what do we do next?"

"I'm going to tighten up the watch on our four suspects," Brian said. "Meanwhile, you'll be safe in the office during the day. When we're ready to spring the trap, you'll start working nights and I'll be here with you."

"What if the killer decides to come to my apartment instead?"

"No, he's an office killer."

"You know the rules and I know the rules," Anne said. "But what if he doesn't know the rules? I need protection. I'm not brave. I'm an editor."

Chapter 34

ANNE WALKED THREE STEPS behind Brian. Then she thought, if the killer was behind them, she would get shot first. But if she moved in front and the killer was waiting for them, she would still get shot first. She moved alongside Brian, thinking that she was much thinner than he was and, therefore, a bad choice as a target.

Brian smiled to reassure her. He pulled the key from his pocket.

"Aren't you going to use your gun?" Anne asked.

"The key usually works," he said.

"What if the killer is waiting for us inside your apartment?"

Brian studied her face and unholstered his gun. "You wait here."

Anne looked up and down the empty hall. "Never mind that," she said. "Give me the gun and you wait out here."

They went in together.

Anne didn't breathe while they searched the apartment. Luckily, it was a small apartment. And they were the only people in it.

"We're okay," Brian said.

"Maybe." Anne stared at the forest mural, the paints and brushes lying on the floor in front of it. "I figured you for a gun collection," she said, "or WANTED posters on the wall. Not this."

Brian grinned. "It's a jungle out there. In here, it's a forest. This is where I get away."

"I need a drink."

Brian fixed two gin and tonics. "Feel safer yet?" he asked.

"You know, for a cop you're not so bad," Anne said.

"For an editor, you're quite a woman."

"Not that I mean anything by it."

"I don't mean anything by anything either," Brian agreed.

"We're not the kind of people who mean anything." Anne smiled at Brian, wondering why she was starting whatever she was starting. Danger, she thought, was like time out from your life. It gave you license to do things you didn't do. She took a step closer.

"That kind of person might think this was a romantic moment," Brian said. "Alone, you, me." It wasn't just that she was long, he thought, it was how far she could reach. He took a step toward her.

"That kind of person is awfully confused." Another step.

They had run out of places to go. He found her mouth and went swimming. She got her hands between them and pushed him away. She backed off, picked up her glass and drank.

"Some people would think that meant I wanted to do it again," she said.

"Some people don't understand how things are."

"That's why they're that kind of people," she said. "I came here for protection. Not romance."

"Protection."

"So come over here and protect my brains out."

Chapter 35

JILLIAN FISSURE SWITCHED ON the tape recorder and set the mike on the table next to her gin and tonic. She shrugged off her robe and stepped into the hot tub. She leaned back, gazed up at the stars shining through the skylight and said, "*Deadly Angel,* chapter two."

She turned on the whirlpool, let the water bubble along her spine, drank some gin, turned off the whirlpool, got out of the hot tub, put a Herbie Hancock disc in the player, got back in the tub and drank some more gin.

"Okay," she said, looking up at the stars. "I'm ready if you're ready. Let's do it." She finished the gin, shut her eyes and started to speak.

" 'We always keep the dressing rooms locked,' the ravishing . . . lovely . . . ravishing but innocent sales girl told the police captain with the flashing brown eyes that looked like two almonds ripening in the Mexican sun . . . the French, the Spanish sun. 'For privacy,' she said . . . she explained.

"The captain took the keys from her and as their hands met, her skin felt like the inside of . . . an oyster . . . a bluepoint oyster that's been kissed by . . . a Maltese lemon.

"The captain opened the door and inside he saw the naked body of Virginia Monroe . . . Hayward, Bacall, Harlow . . . of Virginia Harlow, the richest and most beautiful woman on the island of Manhattan, according to *Vanity Fair,* the magazine which kept track of such vital statistics. To his brown, professional eyes, Virginia looked dead."

Jillian shut off the recorder, feeling good about the work she'd already done, and the night was still young. She knew some writers spent all day working on one paragraph, searching for the perfect words. And they did it in all the worst places. Whereas she had the best writing room in the world.

The room had been a study in their penthouse on the upper East Side. When Jillian needed more room, for that sense of freedom so essential to creative work, she'd had a wall knocked out and incorporated the guest bedroom. Then she had the skylight installed because "one should always write looking up."

The room currently contained the hot tub with whirlpool, an isolation tank, although she hadn't used that in months, an exercycle and a Japanese futon so she could write no matter what her mood called for. There was also an electric typewriter on the L-shaped writing desk, but she never used that, preferring to dictate into one of several tape recorders. Later, a typist would transcribe her drafts and eventually prepare the final manuscript. There were large plants in each corner of the room and 13 pictures of Shakespeare on the walls for inspiration. Shakespeare had replaced Emily Dickinson, who had been preceded by Voltaire, Twain, Dickens, Charlotte Brontë, Hemingway, and Judith Krantz.

Working in such an environment, she had written four mystery novels in twenty months. None of them had been accepted for publication yet, but she knew she was getting close. While she waited for the last one to be accepted, she had begun work on her next book, knowing that the worst thing for her psyche was to wait around to hear from another damn editor. She had to keep writing. It was a compulsion, like a shark has to keep feeding.

Jillian liked that image of the shark. She flipped the tape recorder back on and said, "Note for my Spare Image file: She was like a shark that had to keep feeding or . . . or something."

Jillian mixed another gin and tonic and lay back in the tub, thinking about locked dressing rooms, when the door opened and her husband Todd came in. She sighed. Todd was a good-looking man, unless you had been married to him for several years.

"Do not interrupt me," Jillian said, "unless you have a very good idea of how a beautiful woman is killed inside a locked dressing room at Bloomingdale's."

"You should know everything about what goes on in dressing

rooms at Bloomie's," Todd said. "With the amount of my money you spend there, you should have a room of your own with a name plaque on the door." He turned the volume down on the disc player.

"How tacky," Jillian said. "But not at all surprising."

"What exactly are you doing?" Now he turned the player off altogether.

"I'm writing. I'm creating. I'm staying in touch with my muse, intimate touch. I don't expect you to understand that, with the kind of women you're used to. So run along and amuse yourself. I'm too busy to concern myself with your petty affairs."

"Never mind my affairs." He sat down on the exercycle. "I thought we agreed that unless you sold the last book, you were not going to write them any more."

"I am in the process of selling my last book. That's why I'm getting a jump on the next one, to meet the demand of my future fans."

"That's what you said with the last four books." Todd put his feet on the pedals and spun the wheels. "Every publisher in town has turned you down. All this writing is non-productive."

"That's what they told Jacqueline Susann before she became a mega-seller."

"How do you know what they told Jacqueline Susann?"

"Because if she was a woman, there had to be some man standing by her side, trying his best to cut her down."

Todd spun the wheels hard, then jumped off the exercycle. He drummed his fingers on the isolation tank. "Last year alone you spent five thousand dollars on typing charges. Not to mention twelve hundred for two new tape recorders because the old one made too much noise and distracted you."

"You'll get your money back from my royalties." Jillian sat up high in the hot tub so her breasts floated on top of the water. "You haven't lost a thing."

"If you ever sell a book, which all logical projections indicate you will never do."

"Thanks for the support."

Todd stared at her breasts, wondering how they could share the same body with her brain. "I invest my money in businesses that have a reasonable chance of paying off. That's why I'm successful. If there's one thing I know it's that publishers don't buy books from amateurs like you."

"God, I hate to listen to you." Jillian plunged into the water up to her chin. "It takes all the heart out of my creativity. You disinspire me. Don't you have another business trip to go on?"

Todd sat on the futon, but sank in too far and stood up again. "As I've said before, I'm prepared to finance the publication of one of your books. Then you can say you did it and call it quits."

"It wouldn't be the same," Jillian said. "I have to make it on my own. It only counts if I'm accepted by a major publishing house."

"God, you're nuts," Todd said. "You were nuts when I married you and, despite that great body, you're still nuts."

"Shut up." Jillian's voice was lower than he'd ever heard it. "Or you'll find out what a crazy person can do."

"Either make it or quit."

"I will make it. This time, they're going to publish my book. They have to."

"Why?"

"Because this time I'm not taking no for an answer."

Chapter 36

"THAT'S ME, I SUPPOSE?" Anne leaned against the door and stared at the fawn poised in flight between the trees.

Brian put down his brush and went to her. She wore one of his white shirts, buttoned at the top, hanging loose over belly and thighs. He put his hands inside. "You fell asleep," he said.

"I'm not asleep now," she said. "I want to see you paint." He started to unbutton the shirt. "No, I mean paint paint," she said. "I want to watch you do what you don't let people see you do."

"You have."

"Other women have seen that. I'll bet you never painted for your ex-wife."

"Those weren't my walls."

"Paint for me." She pushed him away.

Brian sat down in the chair and picked up a thin brush. He went to work on the body of the deer. It was a very long deer. Anne stood behind Brian, her legs rubbing against the chair. Then she came and knelt in front of him.

"Art lover," he said.

She straddled him across the chair. He bit the buttons off her shirt.

Later, they tumbled to the floor. Crawled to the couch. He chased her into the shower. She led him back to the bed.

Later still, she opened her eyes and said, "What day is it? What year?"

"It's not," he said.

She went into the kitchen and came back with a glass of ice water. She drank some and poured the rest into his mouth. She lay her head on his chest and he twirled a lock of her hair. "It's been so long for me," she said.

"How long?"

"Months, years."

"Were you sick?"

"I was free," Anne said. "I wanted to live free from the control of men. I needed to prove to myself that I had a choice."

"That's a strange choice to make if you don't have to make it," Brian said.

"Not strange. Just different." He turned her over. "I'm not ready for this," she said.

"Nobody is ever ready for anything," he said. "That's why things happen to people. If it was left up to what people would do for themselves, nothing would ever happen."

Later, he fed her stew from the crockpot and they shared a bottle of cabernet, talking in the low voices of lovers.

"You must drive other men crazy besides me," Brian said. "I don't understand how they could leave you alone for so long."

"I know a lot of writers," Anne said, "but they've all withdrawn from the world. Getting involved with a writer is like hoping a rubber-necker is going to save your life at a traffic accident. Other editors are competition, off-limits. Then there are the publishers for whom I am working, have worked, or will work. Publishers take more of you than you intended to give them. That's why they get rich and you go looking for another job. Not going to bed with them is the only revenge."

"What about men outside the publishing business?"

"I can't do that. They're so real it scares me. I know that I'm not going to be an editor all my life. Sooner or later, my batting average will slip or I'll burn out. I know that's coming. So before I try something easier, like taming lions, I want to do as much as I can here. Relationships don't last. Books last. I want to produce books that people remember."

Chapter 37

When Anne woke in the morning, she was alone, her normal situation. But she was not in her own bed, a completely abnormal condition. She spotted Brian's gun in its shoulder holster, hooked over a chair on his side of the bed. She stretched happily, then looked around to see if anyone was watching.

She pulled the gun from the holster, fanning it across the room. The gun was heavier than she expected. Guns in movies always seemed so light, or people took them so lightly, and in books they weighed nothing at all. Anne slipped her finger in the trigger guard and pretended to shoot ghosts, making soft shooting sounds with her mouth. Then she heard someone approaching the bedroom and hid the gun under the pillow.

Brian came in carrying a breakfast tray of eggs and bacon, toast, and a pot of coffee. "Good morning," he said.

"Don't get mushy and sentimental on me," Anne warned.

"Just an observation." He poured coffee while she tore into the toast. "The eggs aren't mushy either."

"I thought cops always ate out."

"Only at night."

Anne ate some eggs and another piece of toast. She lifted her coffee and looked through the steam at him. "Last night, what happened between us? It was just one of those things, right?"

"Just one of those crazy things."

"It doesn't mean we have to do it again."

"Unless we could find another excuse."

Anne laughed, but she was worried about him. She wasn't sure she could handle a man, much less a hungry one. She finished off the eggs and toast and poured more coffee.

"I'm handing the investigation over to the captain," Brian said. "Let him make the case, if he can."

"But we're so close to solving it."

"The closer we get, the more dangerous it is."

"Danger is how you know you still care about life," Anne said. "Didn't we have this argument in reverse yesterday?"

"That was before last night," Brian said. "If I lost you now, I couldn't go on."

"You big dope. If you lost me, I couldn't go on. You'd have to. Besides, if it weren't for you, I wouldn't be in this mess in the first place."

"If it weren't for me, you'd have a killer stalking you."

"I do have a killer stalking me."

"But you wouldn't know about it if it weren't for me."

"Knowing about it doesn't make me feel any safer," Anne said. "Anyway, I'm not quitting. You want out, I'll catch him myself. But your name comes off the book, and you forfeit your share of the royalties."

"You'll do anything for fame and glory, won't you?"

"You have to. Fame and glory don't come for doing nothing."

Brian shook his head. "If you're going to be stupid, I can't let you do it alone. But there's one thing."

"What now?"

"Give me back my gun."

Anne blushed. She pulled the gun from under the pillow. "I was curious."

"Very." He tossed her clothes to her. She pushed down the covers and started to dress.

"What do we do next?" she asked.

"You'll be safe in your office during the day," Brian said. "There are too many people around for the killer to risk anything. He strikes at night when the editors are working alone. I called the lab while you were asleep, and they finally got the reports back on the fingerprints from the manuscripts. I'm going to pick those up and see if any of our suspects have prior records."

"When will I see you next?"

"I'll meet you in the office this afternoon," Brian said. "But if I'm late for any reason, clear out when everyone else does. Whatever you do, don't work late unless I'm there."

"For more protection?"

"Right."

"Any more protection, I might not be able to walk."

Chapter 38

THE DOOR TO Anne's office opened and Teddy Pendleton stuck his head inside. "Got a sec?" he asked. "I can come back, you're busy?"

"I've always got time for you unless it's business."

"Got an idea," Teddy said. "Could be big. Wanted to run it by you." He took out his notebook.

"Run it," Anne said. Teddy was Everall Publishing's copywriter, responsible for the book jacket copy.

"It's for a book," Teddy said. "The title: *Dead, Dead, Dead, Dead, Dead.*"

"With you so far," Anne said.

"The flap reads: 'Abe Lincoln knew the secret. Now he's dead. So is his dog. Can Dr. Pete and his nephew Billy uncover the secret that could destroy America? Only the ancient sphinx of Egypt holds the answer. And she's not talking.' What do you think?"

"Something's missing," Anne said, "but I can't figure out what."

"It started as a joke," Teddy said. "Then I got to thinking, why not? Why should I always have to come up with something to interest readers in a book after it's been written? Who can pull a pearl out of every oyster? Wouldn't it make more sense to put the pearl in first, then create the oyster around it?"

"It's a whole new approach to books."

"That's it. I write the jacket blurbs first, packed with the good stuff that readers want, and you get a writer to fill in the gaps with words."

"Teddy, you're a fun guy," Anne said. "Let's get together again soon."

"Yeah, you're right." Teddy started for the door. "I think I'm cracking up. Starting to listen to my own ideas."

"You've got a tough job. No doubt about it."

"It's the writers. They get to you after awhile. Maybe I should have my nervous breakdown so I can quit publishing and go into advertising. That's the only thing I'll be good for any more."

"We must talk," Corrine Merks said when Anne answered the phone.

"We are talking," Anne pointed out.

"Good, then you can do something about the cover for Herb's new book." Corrine was a literary agent, and Herb Pennock was her biggest writer, which meant his ten percent paid for more of Corrine's psychiatrist's time than any of her other writers' ten percents. "Herb insisted that I call."

"You are referring to *Killer Chic*?"

"That's the one. Herb is so upset, I can't see straight."

"I've already given Herb cover approval," Anne said. "What else does he want, to draw the cover himself?"

"The naked girl is fine. It's the background color."

"It's blue." Anne searched her in-basket for a proof of the new book cover. She looked at the photo of a naked woman partially concealed by the fur coat she lay upon, set against a solid teal background, what was known in the industry as a Pennock cover. "We do all his covers in teal. It's in his contract."

"I know," Corrine said. "I negotiated the teal clause myself."

"As I recall, teal was his wife's favorite color."

"I know," Corrine said. "I negotiated his marriage contract myself. That's the problem. Marge is out. She's been dropped as Herb's wife. Josephine is in, and she hates teal."

"What color does Josephine like?"

"Magenta," Corrine said. "Josephine and Herb want all his covers to be magenta from now on. They had their colors done, and teal, they found out, is incompatible."

"I'm sure that will make a perfectly hideous cover," Anne said, "which no doubt many of his readers have come to expect from his books. So I'll be glad to change the color, but how do I know this relationship is going to last? The book won't even go on press for three months. What if Herb and Josephine break up and he finds a woman who likes chartreuse?"

"No one said publishing was easy," Corrine said. "All I can tell you is if you can't keep Herb happy, I'm sure someone else can. That's what Herb tells me all the time."

Anne was on her fourth cup of coffee, bent over her desk, proofing galleys when she suddenly felt someone in the office with her. She looked up and saw Rep Gates leaning against the wall, watching her. She dropped her coffee cup. It smashed against the floor with the sound of a gunshot.

"Make you nervous?" Rep asked. He had his arms folded across his chest and leaned at an insolent angle.

"Didn't hear you come in," Anne said.

"People seldom do."

Watch out, Anne thought, he's going to be cryptic. "I'm busy," she said. "What do you want?"

"You know what I want," Rep said.

"Your book? We haven't decided yet. Publishers don't move quickly."

"Make an exception for me."

"Why should I?"

"Because you want to do what's good for you," Rep said. "I'm not the kind of writer you want to cross."

"Are you threatening me?"

"With editors, it's always a hit and miss thing."

"Get out."

"That's not friendly."

"Get out, friend."

Rep took two steps toward her desk. "It didn't work out with Peters and Pryor or with Joss House. I thought maybe you'd realize something they didn't."

"What's that?"

"It's bad to reject me." Rep grinned. "I'm going to make a killing in publishing, one way or the other."

Anne was deep into the gin by the time Brian got to the office with the lab reports. "Any of our would-be writers commit major crimes?" she asked. "Other than bad writing, of course."

"Their prints show that three of them have police records," Brian said. "Dr. Don Dooley was arrested in college for threatening to shoot an English Lit professor."

"I wouldn't call that a crime," Anne said. "Have you ever known an English Lit professor?"

"Dooley pulled a gun on this professor for rejecting his master's thesis."

"Was he convicted?"

"Charges were dropped, and Dooley switched to psychology. Then there's Jillian Fissure," Brian said. "Six years ago, she shot up a country club that rejected her membership. Her husband settled it privately, to avoid scandal."

"The deadly blonde," Anne said. "Have her incarcerated at once. Better yet, take away her American Express card."

"That's exactly what her husband did," Brian said.

"And who is our third criminal?"

"Brigid O'Hare. Twenty-five years ago, she ran with a gang of hoods headed by Teddy 'Big Shoulders' Johnson. She was busted four times for battery, bookmaking, bank robbery, and breaking and entering."

"A regular B-girl."

"No convictions, and nothing since."

"She seemed so sweet, so old."

"This is now. That was then."

"What about Rep Gates? Are you trying to tell me he doesn't have a criminal record?"

"I don't know," Brian said. "That's the problem. The prints the lab got off his manuscript belonged to a woman. She was arrested two years ago for passing bad checks."

"What's her name?"

"Brenda Whitson."

"I know her," Anne said. "She's a manuscript typist. Rep Gates had his book typed. Lots of writers do that so their manuscripts look more professional."

"Then I'm putting Gates back on my list."

"Good, he scares me."

"Why?"

"Because he tries to," Anne said. "He was in here while you were at the lab."

"What did he do?"

"I'm not sure. I think he was making veiled threats that I should publish his book or else."

"Did he produce a weapon or threaten physical violence if you did not comply with his wishes?"

"Not exactly. No, he didn't. God, he was scary." Anne began to cry. Brian wrapped her in his arms. When she got her breath back, she pushed him away.

"I'm okay," Anne said. "I'm all right. This is not going to get to me. I'm a professional, damn it."

Brian didn't know what to do for her. But he knew what to do as a cop. "What was the name of that bar where Gates works?"

"Mac's Place, in the Village."

"I'm going down there to get his fingerprints," Brian said. "Then I'll force the lab to process them right away. I'm going to find out what else this guy has been up to."

"How are you going to get the prints at a bar?" Anne asked.

"Tell you later," Brian said, "when I figure it out."

Chapter 39

BRIAN LEFT THE DELI carrying a bottle of Bud in a paper bag. There was an alley halfway down the block, and he went into it, opened the bottle and poured the beer onto the pavement. A wino lying in a doorway stared at him in disbelief. "This young generation," he muttered. "No respect."

Anne heard the softest rapping at her office door. "Come in," she called.

The door opened slowly, and Brigid O'Hare limped into the office. "I'm still here, thank the Lord," she said.

"You can drop the little old lady routine," Anne said. "I read your book."

"Don't dance around with me," Brigid said, her voice growing tougher. "Did you get it? Did you like it?"

"I was surprised," Anne said. "I figured it would be all tea and poison. I didn't expect a book full of gangland slayings and gun molls."

"I took a writing course," Brigid said. "The teacher said I should write about what I knew best."

"The first time you came in here, you seemed like such a sweet old lady."

"You live long enough, you may end up looking sweet too. I tried to die young and leave a beautiful corpse. But I failed."

"Did you know the gangsters you wrote about in your books?"

"They weren't so hard to know if you were young and liked to have fun," Brigid said. "Most of them are dead now, of course. Cut down in the prime of their miserable lives."

"They were a tough lot, weren't they?"

"They were different from the killers you see today. Now they all have an excuse for what they do: their parents hated them when they were kids, that kind of thing. Of course, their parents hated them. They were rotten, terrible kids. In my day, killers didn't need an excuse. They were a bunch of dirty rats, and they knew it. But enough of this. What's it going to be? You going to publish my book?"

"I'm going to publish one book from an unknown writer," Anne said. "I've narrowed my search to four finalists, and you're one of them."

"Who are the other three?"

"I can't tell you that. It wouldn't be fair."

"Look," Brigid said, "if the other three finalists dropped out, you could declare me the winner and publish my book. Right?"

"Yes, but they want to win as much as you do," Anne said. "They're not going to drop out."

"They could be made to."

Chapter 40

Rep Gates set the Dubonnet down for the blonde and gave the cassis to the redhead. He gave each of them his second-best smile.

He saved his best smile for women who hadn't already fallen. These two had come into the bar looking for him.

Dawn, the blonde, wanted to be a performance artist. She already knew how to perform, and now she was going to City College to learn how to write, in case that might help her create pieces to perform.

Beth, on the other hand, didn't want to be anything. She wanted to experience things. She had already experienced film actors, film directors, film critics, and film professors. A film professor at City College had let it slip that writers often had a considerable influence on film and that Rep Gates, who often let him drink for free, was a writer. Which was how Beth and Dawn ended up in Mac's Place in the Village one afternoon trying to pump Rep about the secrets of writing.

Rep liked the setup, if he could slow the women down so they lasted until he got off duty. The only other problem was the quartet of jerks playing pool in the back room. The jerks kept wanting beer, and Rep was the only one working so they wanted it from him. This Rep considered to be a major distraction, especially since they weren't tipping.

"Our professor said it's hard to make it as a writer," Dawn said.

"Is it hard for you to make it?" Beth asked.

"There's only one thing wrong with being a writer and that's editors," Rep said. "They don't care about writers, only how many books they can sell. Editors make scum look like your best friend. They try to crush writers like me. But I'm not letting them get away with it. I'm fighting back."

As he said that, Rep became aware of a third problem. The problem was walking in the door of Mac's Place. It was that assistant editor from Everall Publishing, Brian Skiles.

Rep put on his best smile and waved Brian over. "We were just talking about the book business," he said. "Look who turns up, one of my editors."

"You mean one of the scum?" Beth asked.

Rep laughed her off. "No, Brian's one of the good guys."

"I'm good scum," Brian leaned toward Rep. "Can we talk in private a minute?"

The women looked offended, but that didn't bother Rep. He pointed to the other end of the bar. "Step into my office."

Brian walked down the bar, looking the place over. The walls of Mac's Place were covered with photos of Greenwich Village life in the 19th century, prints from local artists, posters of prize fights and circuses, and three original abstract paintings that the owner of the bar had bought cheap from a thirsty painter. Mac's Place had changed themes a dozen times in the past six years, with each new theme being layered on top of the last in a never-ending, never-successful quest to turn Mac's Place into one of the Village's hot spots.

"Could I get a Bud?" Brian asked as he settled onto the last stool at the far end of the bar.

"On me." Rep took a Bud from the reefer, poured some into a glass, and set the glass and bottle in front of Brian. "What can I do for you?" he asked.

"I liked your book," Brian said.

Rep felt his heart pound up to primo sex level. Naturally, two of the jerk pool players chose that time to come up and slam some empties on the bar. "More beer, partner," one of them called.

Rep ignored them. "You really liked it?" he asked Brian.

"It has that certain something," Brian said.

"Yo, señor," the second jerk called, "beer here."

"Take care of them," Brian said. "Then we'll talk."

Rep hurried down to get beer for the pool players. While he was gone, Brian emptied the Bud into his glass, holding the bottle by the neck. Then he pulled the paper bag from his jacket, put that empty bottle of Bud on the bar, and slipped the bottle he'd gotten from Rep into the bag. He put the bag away in his jacket and waited.

"So you're going to publish my book?" Rep asked as the pool players carried their beers into the back room.

"It's not that simple," Brian said. "I like your book, but Anne doesn't."

"Then you buy it," Rep said. "Go around her."

"I can't," Brian said. "Not yet anyway. But if I can get her job, you'll be the first writer I discover."

"It's great to finally meet someone who knows what's going on," Rep said. "I'm going to be bigger than Erle, Stanley, and Gardner. If you're on my side, it's going to pay off for you. But those who are against me are going to wish they weren't."

"Right," Brian said. "Look, I've got to go. Just wanted to know where you stood."

After Brian left, Rep strutted down the bar and gave the women his best smile simply because he was feeling good.

"That's it," he told them. "He made me a great offer. I'm going to be big, real big."

"Yeah?" Beth said, "how big can you get?"

"Big enough," Rep said, feeling like he wanted to lean over the bar and bite her.

"Like you're a writer and a bartender," Dawn said. "Does that mean you can do two things at once?"

"Over here, girl-jockey."

The jerks were back, banging more empties on the bar. "More beer, Texas-style," the second jerk said. "This time we want a Lone Star, a Colt Forty-five, and two Pearls."

Rep was feeling his hottest now—sex-hot and mean-hot at the same time. It gave him that furiously lucid ability to get away with anything. He grinned at Beth. "You see what it's like to be a writer and have to work here, casting my pearls before swine."

"Bring some of that swine talk down here, you New York wimpburger," the first jerk said.

"You need to learn some respect for the glorious state of Texas," the second jerk said.

Rep walked down the bar. He grabbed a bottle of long-neck Pearl from the reefer. "You want beer? You got it." He leaned over the bar and cracked the bottle over the first jerk's head.

The guy sat down on the floor and didn't have anything else to say. The second one tried to grab his buddy, while the other two came out of the back room with their pool sticks.

Rep reached under his bar apron and pulled out his gun. "Here I am," he said. "Come get me."

The pool players stopped and raised their hands in the air. Texas cowboys, Rep thought.

Mac, the fat bar owner whose real name was Phil but who let everyone call him Mac because it was easier than changing the name of the joint, came out of his back office, swinging his fat head from side to side, trying to figure out who was threatening to destroy his place today.

"What the hell is going on here?" Mac asked.

"They don't like the service," Rep said.

"No, great service," the second jerk said, holding his dizzy buddy under the arms.

"Really special," the third jerk said.

"Specially him," the fourth jerk said, pointing at Rep with his cue stick.

"They're mistaking me for someone who gives a damn," Rep said.

Mac sighed and put his fat body between the customers and Rep. "Now look, Rep," he began, "I can't have you shooting all my customers. It's bad for repeat business. So how about putting the gun down, and I'll buy everyone a round. Then we'll forget the whole thing. Okay with you, fellas?"

"Okay," the second jerk said.

"We didn't come here for a war," the third jerk said.

"This isn't Texas," the fourth jerk said.

"You see, Rep?" Mac said. "Put the gun away. You don't want to shoot everyone."

"Maybe not everyone," Rep said.

"Sure, it'd be a fulltime job," Mac said.

Rep shrugged and put the gun inside his belt under the apron.

"Good," Mac said. "Now get out. You're fired."

Rep's hand went under his apron again, then he laughed. He didn't need this crap any more. He was one step away from becoming a famous professional successful writer. He ripped off the apron and threw it at Mac. "Screw you all," he said and left with Dawn and Beth.

"We'll take a round of Chivas," one of the jerks told Mac.

"What's this?" Mac said. "I thought you guys were drinking beer."

"If you're buying, we're drinking Chivas."

Out-of-towners, Mac thought. "Get out of here, you deadbeats," he said. "You'll get nothing from me."

The jerk raised his pool stick and Mac slugged him in the face. The jerk fell back against his dizzy buddy, and they both crashed to the floor. Another one hit Mac in the stomach, which didn't impress Mac at all. He picked up a barstool and threw it at the guy.

What the hell, Mac thought, it was time he redecorated again anyway.

Chapter 41

Dr. Don Dooley watched Megan Stennet pacing the carpet back and forth in front of his desk. Her neck was too short, he thought, a fat, inelegant neck, which was probably the root cause of all her psychological problems. At least it was as likely a cause as anything else he had come up with since she'd been his patient.

"I've been coming to you for what, two years?" Megan asked.

Dooley was startled, although he didn't show it, wondering if he was starting to project his thoughts into his patients' minds, using his own mental powers to direct their soft thinking.

"And you've helped," Megan said, not waiting for his response. "I stopped drinking and I got over Paul. Of course, now I have the sleeping pills and Ramone. But that's the way analysis goes."

"The only permanent cure is death," Dooley said. "Everything else is a matter of adjustment."

"Yes, adjustment," Megan said. "My readjusted problem is that I can't sleep at night without the pills, can't sleep at all except in staff meetings. But I just got an adjustment to all that."

"Good, and what is it?"

Megan laughed. "Money is always the best possible adjustment in this the greediest of all possible worlds. Yesterday, I signed a book contract for three big ones."

Some emotion flashed across Dooley's face, but Megan was pacing so hard she missed it. Of course, she hadn't actually looked at Dooley for some months, finding that she could express herself better when she conceived of him as a bodyless voice, something like Oz.

"But you're not a writer," Dooley said.

"What does that have to do with selling books?" Megan asked. "I'm hot, that's what counts. They needed a top woman executive from a Fortune 500 company, and that's me."

"What is the book about?"

"It's an advice book for women. That's the important new category in literature. It's called *How to Succeed in Business Without Going Crazy.*"

"Time's up for today," Dooley said without looking at the clock on his desk.

"That's all right," Megan said. "I've got to go take some publicity photos anyway."

When Megan had left, Dooley locked the door behind her. He unlocked the side door, the door none of his patients had ever been through. Inside the door was a long, narrow room. The wall at the far end of the room was splattered with paint, purples and violets, but mostly reds.

Dooley opened a cabinet and sorted through files of photos until he found a shot of Megan Stennet. He tacked the photo to the wall. Then he went back to the cabinet and took out a paint pellet gas-fired gun. He loaded it with two purple paint pellets and sighted down the barrel at Megan's picture.

"Fake," he said. "Fraud. You couldn't write your way out of a minor neurosis. How can they publish you and not me?"

He squeezed the trigger. The first shot hit low on the wall. He raised his aim and hit Megan right in the mouth. Purple paint splattered across her face.

Dooley took two more photos from the cabinet and hung them on the target wall. He loaded the paint gun with red pellets and shot Anne Baker right between the eyes.

"Damn editors, you're destroying my ego," he said. "I won't let that happen. I deserve my ego. Damn you."

He fired again at Brian Skiles. Red paint dripped down Brian's face, mixing with the paint from Anne's face. He watched the paint drip to the floor. Then he ripped down the photos and threw them away. He stood looking down at the paint, breathing heavily.

When he felt more adjusted, Dooley returned the paint gun to the cabinet, washed his face at the sink and left his target room. He carefully locked the door behind him and pulled on the door knob to make sure it was locked.

Then he walked to his desk, sat down in his deep leather chair, made his face expressionless, and hit the intercom. "You can send in Mrs. Flegel now, Dolores," he said.

Chapter 42

PAM FALCO CONSIDERED her movie star looks to be the biggest hindrance to her career. Pam wanted to be a good cop. The department wanted her to be a crook seducer.

What Brian Skiles wanted her to be was help. He caught up with her in the Riverside squadroom. "I need your help," he said.

"That's a line I've heard before," Pam said. "What guy do you want me to shimmy up to?"

"Murder suspect. I think he'll talk to you."

Pam looked up from the reports stacked on her desk. "I'm the kind of woman guys always think other guys will talk to."

"Look, I don't know you, but they say you're good," Brian said. "I need someone who's good. Can you help me?"

Pam thumped the stack of reports. "Right now, I'm busy with a few other investigations. Of course, you ask me next week, I'll be busy with a few other investigations. Always am. Ever since they put me in plain clothes, although plain clothes is not exactly what I get to wear."

"I don't care what you wear," Brian said.

"Every time some detective has a guy he thinks will rattle his teeth at something flashy, he comes to me. I can't even get a date because I'm too busy dating guys for other cops."

"You want to help me crack a murder case? That's going to look good on your record."

"My record already looks good. I get lots of credit, lots of requests. What I don't get is a promotion to a different assignment. I got typecast early, the seducer, and that's all they think I'm good for. It's because of the way I look. It's not fair."

"I'm sorry you're not ugly," Brian said, "but there's nothing I can do about it. I only have one thing to offer you."

"What would that be?"

"I'm going to catch a killer," Brian said. "If that means anything to you, then help me. If not, I'll find some other way."

"All right, don't go moral on me," Pam said. "I'll give you one night. If the guy wants to talk right away, fine. If he is the strong, silent type who wants to have his resistance broken down, sorry, I'm too busy working other guys."

"Don't worry about this guy. He wants to talk. He wants to tell everyone his story."

"Where do I find him?"

"Mac's Place in the Village. He tends bar there. Name's Rep Gates."

"And what do you want me to squeeze out of him?"

"Rep thinks he's a writer, a novelist. But no one else does. All the editors keep rejecting him. I want you to find out how mad he is about all those rejections."

"You mean, is he mad enough to kill."

"That's what I mean," Brian said.

"What a weird way for a person like me to be a cop," Pam said. "I do everything a hooker does, except for one thing."

"What's that?"

"Make good money."

When Brian finished briefing Pam Falco, he checked with the desk sergeant on the whereabouts of Detective Pete Crill.

"Try the weight room," the sergeant suggested. "Pete's got some idea that biceps are going to help solve cases."

Brian went down to the basement and followed his nose into the weight room. Pete Crill was lying on a bench press, puffing hard at 100 pounds. "Spot for me, huh?" he asked.

Brian stepped behind the bench and guided the bar as Pete lifted. Pete did three reps, sat up and wiped his forehead on his sleeve. "Do me a favor," Brian began.

"No, you do me a favor," Pete interrupted, "don't ask me for a favor."

"I've got too many suspects," Brian said. "I need you to follow two of them for me."

"Why?"

"So I can find out where they go, what they do," Brian said. "It's a little trick those of us who work in the police business call surveillance."

"Yeah, but why should I do it when I can easily occupy my time with the low-life I call my own?"

"It's the book murder," Brian said.

"You mean those editors who got shot up? No way, pal, that belongs to his majesty, Captain Stark. And what I heard is he took you off the case."

"I'm going after something he won't touch," Brian said. "The real killer."

"Why?"

"Because I'm right and he's wrong."

"That's always been your problem, Brian. You think being right counts for something around here. You want to fight the captain, that's your business. Me, I want to make pension."

"Two women, that's all," Brian said. "You follow one, then you follow the other. No intervention. And the second one is old. She can't move fast."

"The last time I did you a favor, I almost got killed."

"The last time, I saved your life."

"You wouldn't have had to save my life if you hadn't put it in jeopardy in the first place."

"Pete."

"Brian." Pete started to lift the bar again, then gave up. "Where does a guy go to trade his friends for enemies? What do you want me to do?"

Brian told him.

Chapter 43

ERIN HAD EATEN exactly half her Chicken Elliot when she pushed the plate away and asked Bissie, "You remember that football player you were dating last week?"

Bissie, whose diet called for her to eat every other day but then as much as she wanted, eyed the second half of Erin's Chicken Elliot, having already polished off her own Veal Mark. "The one I met when I did the beer commercial?"

"I saw that on TV the other night," Anne said. "You did a great smile."

"I had a longing look too," Bissie said, "but it ended up on the cutting room floor. You going to eat the rest of that, Erin?"

"He keeps calling me up for a date." Erin pushed her plate away. On her diet, she ate every day but only half a meal.

"Then he has learned to dial a phone?" Bissie said. "You can have him if you want him. He's too stupid for me."

"That's why I want him," Erin said. "I'm tired of smart, sensitive men. The big guy may be stupid, but at least you don't have to waste so much time relating to him."

"The guy I really went for was the director of the commercial," Bissie said, "even though he cut out my longing look. But he only wants to make it if you let him videotape it for his personal collection. That's sick."

"You ever notice how every time we get together, all we talk about are jobs and romance?" Anne said.

"I'd like to talk about the national debt," Erin said, "but I can never seem to stay awake long enough to do it."

"Besides, Erin and I talk about the men," Bissie said. "You talk about business."

"Maybe," Anne said, finishing her martini and signaling the waiter for another.

"What are you getting at, Anne?" Erin asked, signaling the waiter to make it two. "Oh no, I don't believe it. Do you believe it, Bissie? I don't."

"What?" Bissie held up three fingers. "What?"

"Don't you get it?" Erin said. "She did it. The famous Anne Baker slept with someone."

"How could she sleep with someone?" Bissie asked. "The famous Anne Baker is celibate."

The waiter set down three martinis and cleared the plates. "Are we thinking of exploring desserts today?" he asked. "Chef has been doing some fascinating things with whipped cream."

"I don't think we're going to need dessert today," Erin said. When the waiter cleared out, she asked, "Who was it?"

"Brian Skiles," Anne said. "The cop."

"You slept with a cop?" Erin said. "What, at gunpoint?"

"It was something we had to do," Anne said. "I've edited hundreds of books where someone sleeps with the cop sooner or later. Last night, it was my turn."

"God, I love romance," Bissie said. "Did he realize how honored he was after all this time you spent celibate?"

"Who knows?" Anne said. "He's a man."

"How did you do it, after being away from it for so long?"

Anne shrugged. "It's like falling off a bicycle, except you don't skin your knees."

"I have," Bissie said. "My knees, I mean."

"So what was it like after all this time?" Erin asked.

Anne blushed. "It was like being on a diet for too long. Then one night you find yourself in Paris and all the restaurants have a reservation in your name. You don't want to be a glutton, but you can't say no to anything."

"I can't stand it." Erin looked around the dining room. "I wish there was a good-looking guy here right now."

"What about the waiter?" Bissie suggested.

"No, I wouldn't want to end up on the menu here, being explained to strangers," Erin said. "Now that you've had a man again, Anne, welcome back."

"I had a man last night," Anne said. "That doesn't mean I still have him."

"What went wrong?"

"Nothing. He's a cop and I'm an editor."

"I thought he was a man and you were a woman," Bissie said.

"That may be true at three in the morning," Anne said. "But mostly we live nine to five."

"What's the problem?" Bissie asked.

"I'm scared," Anne said. "He's using me."

"Men," Erin said in disgust.

"I mean as a trap to catch a killer."

"How romantic," Bissie said.

"Not if the killer wins," Anne said.

"Then why let him use you like that?"

"I'm using myself in the same way," Anne said. "That's what frightens me. I want to write a best-seller, and I'm willing to risk my life to do it. Sometimes, I think I'm crazy."

"Other times you worry that you're not," Erin said.

Chapter 44

BRIGID O'HARE SAT in her apartment, drinking, thinking, looking out the window, seeing 1952, the time Pecs and Country took on four sailors who had tried to pick up her and Babs at the Glitter Club over on the West Side, 26th, 27th, something like that.

The doorbell had been ringing for five minutes before she heard it. Brigid got up, kicked aside some newspapers and opened the door.

An old man stood there, wrinkled face, flattened nose, liver spots on his forehead, but the same steely blue eyes he'd had when he used to kill people for a living.

"That you, Cheeks?" Brigid asked. "Cheeks Morantz?"

"How you been, Brig?"

"For sixty years I've not complained," Brigid said. "I won't start now."

"Me, I got arthritis," Cheeks said. "Can hardly hold a gun any more."

"So who asked?"

"Yeah. Can I come in or what?"

Brigid backed away from the door, and Cheeks followed her into the apartment, walking with a limp. Brigid pushed some magazines, books, and an empty can of cat food off a chair so Cheeks could sit down. She took the other chair.

"Look, I'll get right to it," Cheeks said.

"I've been waiting," Brigid said.

"Yeah. The boys don't want you writing about them."

"Who says I am?"

"We heard you were writing a book, and we figured what else you got to write about, a diet book?"

"Most of the boys are dead anyway," Brigid said. "What should they care?"

"They got kids, don't they? Kids who are decent in their communities."

Brigid laughed, a harsh rattle. "Communities? We used to have neighborhoods."

"No neighborhoods any more," Cheeks said, rubbing the pain in his leg that hadn't gone away for ten years. "Now it's housing developments, shopping malls, aerobics classes."

"They can have it."

"They do. But it's not easy for the kids to be respectable if someone's writing about how their old man used to be a gangster. A guy could get himself kicked out of the PTA for that."

"What do you want from me?" Brigid sighed. First the guys who were dead wanted stuff from her. Now the guys who were sort of alive wanted other stuff from her.

"Don't publish that book," Cheeks said.

Brigid laughed, her laugh suddenly young and clear again. "Leave it to a hood to try and stop me from doing something I can't do anyway."

"Don't make us get tough with you, Brigid."

Brigid walked over to the refrigerator and opened it. "You don't scare me, Carl. Carl Morantz. I'll kill anyone who tries to stop me from publishing my book." She pulled a gun out of the refrigerator and pointed it at him. Cheeks stared at the gun, and the pain in his leg went away for the first time in ten years. "Now get out of here before I use you for target practice," Brigid said.

Cheeks got up and walked to the door, his limp gone. "Okay, Brigid," he said, "have it your way."

Chapter 45

As soon as Pam Falco walked in the joint, she knew it wasn't Rep Gates behind the bar. This bartender was fat and old. He looked her over, wondering if she was a hooker. No one ever thought she was a cop.

"Help you?" the bartender asked.

"Isn't Rep working tonight?"

"Gates, that crazy bastard. Pulled a gun on me. I had to take it away from him and throw him out. You a friend of his?"

"Know where he is now?" Pam asked.

"You throw someone out down here, they never go far. He's working at the X-Spot, across the street. Hope he starts shooting up the joint. Drive the customers back here."

Pam wasted a smile on him and went across the street. The X-Spot was more like it, for her taste, a mix of art deco and post-punk modern. There wasn't much business despite the hip look, two guys down at the end of the bar, a couple in one of the booths and Rep Gates behind the plank.

She took a stool at the bar and ordered a white wine. "Haven't seen you in here before," Rep said as he set the glass on a napkin in front of her. He wore jeans and a Hawaiian shirt that showed off his arm muscles well. He looked okay to Pam, but since she was a cop, looks didn't mean a thing to her.

"I'm changing scenes," she said. "I got tired of hanging out in those theater bars with all the other out-of-work actors. I've got to find something to change my luck."

"You're an actress?" Rep leaned over the bar. This, he thought, is what an actress should look like.

"That's what I say," Pam said. "Producers, they don't necessarily agree with me. To them, I'm just someone getting in their way."

"I know what you mean," Rep said. "Have another? It's on me."

She looked up at him, as if seeing him for the first time, as if they were both now figuring out what they were going to do for the rest of the night. "All right," she said. "First good offer I've had in months."

Rep poured her wine and a scotch rocks for himself. "You been in anything?" he asked.

"I've been in New York trying to make it for eleven months now. It's bad luck for an actress to go into her second year without a part. I do six, seven auditions a week. Everything I can find: Broadway, Off, Off-Off, soaps, commercials. In eleven months, I've gotten a dozen call-backs. Besides that, nothing but rejections."

"This world is paved with rejections," Rep said. "Rejection is like an automatic response for them."

"It's not because I'm not good, because I am good," Pam said, slurring her words. "I was the best actress in my home town anyone ever saw; they all said so. Here, they won't give me a chance. Give me another drink, will you? They're driving me mad. I don't know what to do. It's the producers. Who made them God? Who gave them the right to reject me? I'd like to get even just once."

"Who wouldn't?" Rep gave her another wine, thinking that it had already been decided what they would do with their night, as soon as he could close up anyway. "The reason they get away with it is because you play by their rules."

"Last I heard, it's their game and they get to make the rules."

"That's what they want you to think," Rep said. "Look, you go to an audition and they reject you. Then what do you do?"

"Find another audition and try again."

"That's where you make your mistake," Rep said. "When they reject you, you accept it. If you didn't agree to be rejected, they couldn't get away with rejecting you. There'd be no way."

"There's an interesting idea." Pam drank some wine, spilling a little as she put the glass back on the bar. "What am I supposed to do about it?"

Rep wiped up the wine with the bottom of his apron. "That's the tricky part. That's where you've got to think and plan and figure out how to unreject yourself."

"Oh, great."

"Look, if it was easy everyone would do it."

Pam swayed on her bar stool. "Maybe you've got an idea could help me?"

Rep pushed back from the bar. He checked his other customers, then shook his head. "No, you've got to do it on your own. But once you believe you can do it, you'll find a way. Look, I'm closing up early. If you really want to change your luck, I live a couple blocks from here."

"Right, sure." Pam pushed herself off the stool, wobbled and looked around for the women's room. "I've got to, you know." She weaved to the back of the bar, figuring she had gotten from Rep all that Brian Skiles had any right to expect.

In the bathroom, she took some white powder from her purse and rubbed it under her eyes, making her look like something had died. She splashed water on her blouse, as if she'd had to wash something off it.

When she came back out, she held her head in her hands. She looked at Rep, embarrassed and sick. "I lost it," she said. "Too much to drink."

"Yeah, right." Rep had seen this all before, had cleaned it up too many times. He was more concerned that she hadn't made it to the bowl than that they wouldn't make it at all. Shame to see a nice body treated like that, though.

"I have to get home and sleep," Pam said. "But I owe you one. The next time, it'll be on me."

Chapter 46

FIRST, BRIAN NEVER should have gone into the bar. Kitty's Corner was where he and Cathy had hung out during their first exciting year of marriage. No, during their first year of marriage, the exciting one. Kitty's Corner had blue lights and warm booths, and lovers went there. Not ex-lovers.

Second, Brian shouldn't have started drinking boilermakers. Third, he shouldn't have kept drinking them.

Old places belonged to old times and you should never go back there, he thought as he ordered a refill from the bartender. He heard the smoky laughter of lovers from the booths. You felt cheated that new people were there, having new times, totally unaware of what you'd done there when you were in love.

They were building toward their own old times, Brian thought in consolation, only they didn't know it because they were so busy enjoying what they were doing as they did it.

Places like this should close up when you broke up. The past should not go on.

Brian drank half the whiskey and chased it with beer. At the end of the bar, a couple of guys were watching the game on the TV. But the Knicks were behind by twenty in the third, and Brian couldn't bear it. He didn't want to push for a comeback that wasn't going to work out in the end.

Like Cathy. His tape wouldn't stop her for long. The only way to stop her was to give her what she wanted. Go back with her. She wouldn't keep him for long. She'd go on to something else, and he could go back to being a cop.

The hell with that, he thought. He signaled the bartender.

But what was Anne offering him? First of all, she hadn't offered him anything. She had slept with him one night because she was scared. Fear was not the foundation of a lasting relationship.

Not that he wanted one with Anne Baker. She was nothing but another Cathy. Funnier maybe, and longer, but just as manipulative, just as career-threatening.

Besides it wasn't a choice between Cathy and Anne. It was Cathy or nothing. Anne or nothing.

And Anne would lead to nothing. For all he knew, she was lying across her desk right now with Brandon Everall inside her. Or a bullet.

Don't fall in love with a victim, he thought. But the long, thin people of the world were set up to break. They were brittle. Anne's only weapons were her words. How sharp they were, and yet could not cut.

Anne was depending on him to save her, but there was no such thing as police protection. That's what a cop told a potential victim when he wanted her to sit still and play decoy for him so he could get off a good shot at the killer.

If a killer wanted to murder you, sooner or later you were dead. You could be surrounded by cops 24 hours a day, and the killer would still get to you. Oswald and Sirhan and Ray and Hinckley and the Mafia had proven that. A highly motivated killer could not be stopped, except through sheer good luck.

What a cop was good at, if he was a good cop, was catching the killer afterwards. That's why cops liked decoys. It gave them a target, a place to start.

Most killers wouldn't work as hard to get away with their crimes as Brian would work to catch them. Killers were willing to take their chances because eliminating their victims was their overwhelming objective. Escape was secondary.

For killers, getting away with murder was only job two. For Brian, catching the killer was job one. That gave him the only advantage he had.

But where, he wondered as he downed the last of his whiskey, was love on that list? He knew where Cathy was, but where was Anne?

The bartender looked over at Brian and pointed at his empty glass. Brian shook him off and forced himself to head for the door.

Chapter 47

"You know what we have to do today, don't you?" Brian asked Anne as they drank their morning coffee in her office.

"I'm not going to like this, am I?"

"They're going to like it less," Brian said. "We have to reject them."

"All four?"

"Yes. We've pumped up their hopes of getting published. Now we have to shatter them, to force the killer's hand."

"But three of them are innocent," Anne said.

"They all wanted to be writers," Brian said. "This goes with the territory."

"Now you're an editor."

An hour later, Brian stood behind Anne while she faced Dr. Don Dooley across her desk. "This is the worst book I've ever read," she told him.

Dooley's face remained expressionless. He folded his arms across his chest and asked, "Why are you so hostile?"

"Someone has to tell you the truth," Anne said. "You'll never be a writer." She handed the manuscript back to him.

Dooley, still without expression, stood up. The chair lifted with him because he had not let go of the arms. He unclenched his fists, and the chair dropped to the floor. "We'll decide what to do about my book when you can relate in a more positive way," he said. Slowly, calmly, he left the office.

An hour later, Anne was telling Jillian Fissure the same story. "I'd never publish your book," she said. "It's stupid and you're a dreadful writer. Give it up."

Jillian stood up and looked down at Anne. "You silly, little, odd-looking person," she said. "You don't have what it takes to stop me. My God, look at your clothes."

Next came Rep Gates. He refused to sit down, but stood opposite Anne and Brian, his handsome eyes furious.

"You'll never be a writer," Anne began.

"Don't give me that," Rep said. "I warned you not to play games with me."

"I'm not going to do anything with you," Anne said. "Take that thing you call a book and get out."

Rep leaned across the desk and stuck his face up close to Anne's. "You had your chance," he growled. As he straightened up, he nodded to Brian, then slammed the door on the way out.

Finally, Brigid O'Hare shuffled into the office, looking neither so old nor sick, but tired. She knew they were going to reject her as soon as she walked into the office. It was exhausting to get her hopes up for nothing.

"Your book is simply not any good," Anne said. "You can't write and the story isn't believable. You've wasted too much of my time already, playing on my sympathy. Give it up."

Brigid sighed. She didn't look at Anne, nor at Brian. There was no reason to look at them any more. She picked up her manuscript and trudged to the door, growing more tired with each step. She didn't even have the energy to close the door as she left.

"Excuse me," Anne said to Brian. She shut the door softly, then went into the store room, picked up every book on the shelf and threw them against the wall, one at a time.

Brian decided the best thing to do was leave her alone. He took out his gun, unloaded it and reloaded it. After five minutes, the thumping from the closet ceased and Anne came back out.

"Well," she said. "I didn't have to be an editor. I could have been a Broadway producer.

Brian went to her and opened his arms. She brushed past him. "Anne," he started.

"I know. I'm a professional. You're a professional, although you need a gun to do what I can do with a few words: destroy people's lives. Nevertheless, let us conduct ourselves like professionals and screw the world. What next?"

Brian sighed. "Next, we go about our business and wait for tonight. And if not tonight, then we wait for tomorrow night. It's up to the killer now. We've done all we can do."

Chapter 48

Jillian Fissure walked down Fifth Avenue looking in the shop windows. Detective Pete Crill walked down Fifth Avenue looking at Jillian Fissure. He had never tailed anyone who looked that good.

But the woman did nothing but shop, which was not one of Pete Crill's favorite activities. In fact, if he couldn't buy something within 90 seconds, he didn't buy it at all.

As Jillian entered a fancy dress shop, Pete crossed the street. He saw Jillian through a window that was as wide as the store. She was looking through dresses on a rack, holding them up in front of her and gazing into the mirror. A clerk came up and offered to help, which seemed unnecessary to Pete since Jillian was a very professional shopper.

There were three phone booths on Pete's side of the street, and one of them was actually working. He decided to check in with Brian Skiles while Jillian browsed. Only when Pete called Skiles' number, a woman informed him that Brian wasn't there.

"Take a message?" Pete asked. "When Skiles gets back, tell him this Jillian Fissure has been shopping for three hours now. Tell him that's more shopping than I've done with my wife in fifteen years. Tell him . . ."

Pete never told her what to tell him because the store clerk pointed to the rear of the store and Jillian moved off toward a door marked Exit.

"Got to run," Pete said into the phone. He ran across the street as Jillian left by the back door.

As Pete ran into the store, the clerk stepped toward him, still holding a dress Jillian had given her. "Can I help you, sir?"

"Got that in my size?" Pete said as he trotted to the rear of the store.

Pete pulled open the back door and saw he was coming out into some kind of alley. Jillian must have spotted him somehow and now she was making her break. He stepped out into the alley and saw a blur.

The blur hit Pete Crill flush in the face and knocked him off his feet. Pete's face went numb as he lay on his back, stunned, unable to move. He stared up at the blur and saw that it was the lid to a garbage can.

Pete tried to get up, but he couldn't move. He looked beyond the garbage can lid and saw who was holding it: Jillian Fissure. She dropped the lid next to his head. He flinched, trying to force his arm to get his gun by sheer will power. Nothing happened except for the sweat pouring down his face.

Jillian lifted a high-heeled boot and pushed his jacket open with her toe. She looked at the gun in his shoulder holster.

"Tell my husband," she said, "if he's going to have me followed, he should hire a dick who can do the job better. I've been on to you for hours."

Jillian bent down, pulled the gun from Pete's holster and put it in her purse. He made his arm move and grabbed one of her boots. She kicked him in the face with the other one.

These private eyes were such amateurs, she thought as she walked away down the alley.

Chapter 49

REP GATES WORKED over the punching bag in his loft, steady one-twos broken by bursts of vicious right hooks. He was sweating hard, stripped to the waist and snorting through clenched teeth. Finally, he tore off the gloves and threw them at the typewriter. In the shower, he turned on the cold full-force and made himself stand there for five minutes. Then he dressed, slipped the pistol into his pocket, and left the loft.

Brian Skiles was sitting low in his car wondering if he shouldn't be staking out Dr. Don Dooley's office instead, when Rep Gates came out onto the street.

Rep walked to the bus stop at the corner. Brian slipped down behind the wheel and didn't move until Rep got on a bus. Then he followed the bus uptown, where Rep got off two blocks from the offices of Everall Publishing.

Brian parked the car in front of a fire hydrant, flipped up his police sticker on the visor and followed Rep on foot. Rep stopped across the street from Everall and stepped back into a doorway.

Brian watched from his own doorway, but Rep made no move. Five minutes later, Anne Baker exited the office building and walked down the street. Rep followed her. Brian followed him.

Anne walked uptown two blocks and went into Sam's Bar and Grill. Rep peered into the window, then trotted across the street and found another doorway. Brian had already found his own on the same side of the street. They both waited.

Three minutes later, a cab pulled up in front of Sam's and Dr. Don Dooley got out. He went into the bar.

Anne was already on her second martini when she saw Dooley searching for her among the dim booths. She made no move to help him find her.

"There you are," he said, slipping in across from her. "Thank you for meeting me here."

"I haven't done anything yet," Anne said, "aside from giving the barkeep practice in making bad martinis."

"I want to change your mind," Dooley said.

"I figured as much." A bored waitress slouched up to their booth and waited. "Another of these exceptional martinis," Anne said. "Tell your pal to keep plugging away. He'll get it yet."

"Make it two," Dooley said. "On me." The waitress slouched away, unimpressed by either of them. Dooley leaned across the table. "You have to publish my book."

"Do I? Why?"

"I've already told everyone that I'm a writer," Dooley said. "Now I simply must have a book to prove it."

"You should talk less and write more," Anne said. "That's what real writers do."

"We can work it out so it pays off for both of us."

"Can we?"

The waitress brought their martinis. Dooley paid her and waited till she went away before he spoke, although he could have told her about his plans to blow up Manhattan and she couldn't have cared less.

"Look," Dooley said to Anne, "let's say you bought my book for twenty thousand dollars."

"All right," Anne said, "let's."

Dooley sat back and smiled. He spread his hands wide. "Don't you see how this works out for both of us? You buy the book for twenty, and I'll give half of it back to you. A fifty-fifty split. What do you say?"

Across the street from Sam's Bar and Grill, Rep Gates checked his watch. He shook his head and walked swiftly out of the doorway.

From his own doorway down the block, Brian Skiles watched Rep leave and didn't know who to stay with. He reached inside himself for an instinct, wasn't sure he had gotten one, but followed Rep anyway.

Melanie Armatraz was locking up the outer door of the editorial offices of Everall Publishing when someone grabbed her from behind. She screamed and dropped the keys.

"Love that scream," her attacker said.

Melanie turned and saw it was Rep Gates. She laughed and opened her mouth for his kiss.

"You scared me," she said a few minutes later.

"That's only the beginning of what I'm going to do to you," Rep said. He knelt to pick up the keys and ran his hands up under her skirt. "Tonight, it's your fantasy."

As Melanie and Rep walked to the elevator, Brian Skiles watched them from the end of the corridor.

Anne Baker sat at her desk, pleasantly woozy from four martinis. Brian paced in front of the desk, glancing too often out the window as the sky turned dark.

"What were you talking to Dr. Dooley about?" Brian asked.

"He tried to bribe me to publish his book," Anne said. "Offered me a kickback on the advance. Plus free psychoanalysis. I think he was getting to the set of knives when I left."

"A lot of writers try that?"

"Some."

"Does it work?"

"Not with me."

"Why not?"

Anne shrugged. "If I was in it for the money, I'd get out. Find myself a real job. I'm here for the books. Create a book, touch eternity."

The door to the office swung open. Brian pivoted, his hand going into his jacket. Brandon Everall sauntered into the office, looking decidedly jaunty and darkly tanned. Brian wished he had shot him anyway.

"Working late again tonight?" Brandon asked. "Alone together?"

"I'm just leaving," Brian said.

"I'm just getting started," Anne said.

"Good," Brandon said. "No point the two of you getting in each other's way." He turned back to the door, then stopped. "Look, Anne, I have to go out and pick up a manuscript I've decided to buy. When I get back, we'll discuss something important—your future here."

"Now what do you think he meant by that?" Anne asked, after Brandon left.

When she opened her eyes, Melanie Armatraz saw her breasts

reflected in the dreamy glow of the brass headboard of her bed. Lovely breasts, she thought, and arched her back so they stood higher. Melanie could also see the red silk scarves that bound her wrists and ankles to the brass bed.

Rep Gates sat next to her, stroking the insides of her legs. Melanie stretched and purred. Rep pressed a finger between her teeth, and she licked it. He pulled her hair back until her chin came up, then kissed her neck.

"If your mysteries are half as good as your love-making," Melanie said, "you're going to be another Alfred Hitchcock."

Rep grinned. He kissed each of her breasts, then got off the bed. He walked into the other room and started to dress.

"Hey, loverboy," Melanie called from the bedroom. "Come back in here and untie me. There's something I want to do to you."

"Be right there," Rep said.

Melanie's purse was hooked over the closet doorknob. Rep opened the purse and found the keys to Everall Publishing's editorial offices. He put the keys in his pocket and left Melanie's apartment.

Melanie lay on the brass bed, waiting for Rep to come back to her. She thought she heard the front door close. She struggled against the scarves that bound her. "Undo me, you bastard," she shouted.

Chapter 50

ANNE BAKER KEPT EDITING because that's what an editor did. She refused to glance out the office window, although she knew the sky was black with night. The heater was off again and it was cold in the office, but she didn't feel that. But she did hear the key open the door. She looked up from her desk and saw Rep Gates standing inside her office, jangling keys in his left hand.

"Scared you again," he said.

Anne looked at Rep's right hand. It was empty. She looked again at his left; the keys dangled like small, serrated knives. "This office is closed," she said, the words coming out like the panting of an exhausted runner. "What do you want?"

"You rejected me," Rep said. "I don't like that."

Anne shrugged. "Nothing personal."

Rep grinned. "Other editors rejected me, and guess what happened to them?"

"They felt good?"

"Not for long." Rep reached inside his leather jacket and pulled the gun from his belt. He pointed it at Anne and moved forward. "I'm giving you one more chance to . . ."

"Drop the gun." Brian Skiles jumped out of the storage closet and pointed his gun at the middle of Rep's back. "Drop it or you'll never write again."

Rep giggled and opened his hand. His gun fell to the floor. Anne nearly fell off her chair. "Since when do editors pack guns?" Rep asked.

"I'm a cop," Brian said. "And you're under arrest."

"What for?"

"Murder. Up against the wall."

Rep nodded his head and leaned against the wall. When Brian cuffed his hands behind his back, Rep started laughing. Brian had seen other people have strange reactions to getting arrested, so he paid no attention to Rep.

"You okay?" Brian asked Anne.

Anne was holding onto her desk with both hands. "Fine."

"I have to book him at the station," Brian said. "You want to come along?"

Anne shook her head, then put her hands over her ears to stop it from shaking. She took a deep breath. "You go ahead. I want to stay here and finish our book. If we move fast, we can have the book ready by the trial. It will make great publicity."

"You sure you're okay?"

"This is my office," Anne said. "I work here. I'm fine."

Brian took a step toward Anne, looked at Rep and stepped back. "I guess this is where most people would say goodbye."

"I guess they would," Anne said.

"I guess I'm going to puke," Rep said. "Can we hurry it up?"

Brian pushed Rep's face into the wall. "Shut up, you. I'll arrest you when I'm good and ready." Rep started laughing again. "What are you laughing about?"

"You don't get it, do you?" Rep said. "Getting arrested is the best thing that ever happened to me. I finally got it made as a writer. All the publishers in town are going to bid big bucks for my story. Now I can reject you."

Rep kept laughing as Brian walked him out of the building, shoved him in the car and drove away.

Chapter 51

ANNE WATCHED FROM the window as Brian's car drove away, wondering if she would ever see him again. At the trial, she thought, at the book signings. But never alone again, never intimate; there was no more reason for that.

She didn't want to think about those things. She wanted to become what she had been before her office was violated. She poured some gin and sat down at her typewriter.

"I was working late in the office," she wrote. But something was bothering her. She stopped typing and listened. There was a soft knocking from the lobby. She decided to ignore it and turned back to her work. Her hands poised over the keys, but she couldn't ignore the small, steady taps on the lobby door.

She jumped up and went into the lobby. Through the smoky

glass of the outer door, she saw a short, fat cleaning woman holding a broom and dustpan. "We're closed," Anne said. "Go away."

"No, no, I clean up," the cleaning woman said through the door. Anne looked down for a mouse because the cleaning woman had the same Russian accent as Django, the Mickey killer.

"Don't need to," Anne said. "We're already clean."

"Must do job," the cleaning woman insisted. "Lost key."

So that's how Rep got the key to the office, Anne thought. Simple, yet deadly.

"In please. Can't lose job. Clean fast, clean hard."

Anne sighed. "I'm plagued by janitors." She unlocked the door and swung it open.

Brigid O'Hare dropped the broom and pointed a gun at Anne's stomach. She also dropped the accent. "I've come to clean up," she said, "and it won't take long. Move back now." Brigid stepped inside and shut the door behind her.

Anne shook her head. "But we already caught the book killer."

Brigid laughed. "Two or three times from what I hear. Cops today are as dumb as they were in my day." She motioned with the gun, holding it loosely like a person who was used to handling guns. Anne walked back into her office. Brigid came in behind her and shut the door.

"Why have you been killing editors?" Anne asked.

"Why not?"

"You don't kill people without a reason."

"They rejected me. You rejected me. Soon life will reject me."

"That's not true," Anne said, having no idea what she meant since it obviously was true.

"No one wants to hear what an old lady has to say," Brigid said. "They think I'm stupid because I'm old. But I'm not."

"You can't kill people for being insensitive," Anne said. "My God, there'd be no one left."

But Brigid wasn't listening. "I was tough when I was young," she said, "and I'm still tough. Before I go, I'm making myself feel better by taking some of my enemies with me."

"I'm not your enemy."

Brigid stared at her. "You're not in my gang," she said.

"They'll catch you sooner or later."

"What can they do to me? Give me life? I'm not going to live long enough for life."

Anne found herself running out of arguments for the first time in her life. That made her mad. "Don't you want to get your book published?"

"That's all I want any more," Brigid said. "You have no idea what that would mean to us. But no one will do it. So you die. That's the way it goes with my gang." She raised the gun.

"No, wait," Anne said. "I'm going to give it to you. I'll publish your book."

"Too late."

"It's not too late," Anne said. "We can sign the contract right now. You name the price, I'll pay it."

"Sure, then you'll have me arrested and tear up the contract."

"Of course, I'll have you arrested," Anne said. "But that guarantees I won't tear up the contract. Think of the publicity. Book killer turns out to be little old gangster lady. Guaranteed best-seller. We'll make millions."

Brigid had heard people plead for their lives before and she knew you were never supposed to believe them. Still . . .

"It'll be the best deal either of us ever made," Anne said.

"Maybe . . ."

"We'll sign the contract right now," Anne said. "I've got one in that desk." She pointed to Brian's desk behind Brigid.

Brigid shook her head and kept the gun between them. "You stay back. I'll get it myself."

"It's in the top drawer," Anne said.

Brigid pulled the top drawer open. It came off in her hand, throwing her off-balance. She fell over backward and hit the floor hard. The gun slid across the room.

Anne went for the gun, but Brigid pulled on her ankles and tried to kick her. Anne rolled away.

The two women faced each other. She's old, Anne thought, she can't fight. She's not strong enough.

Brigid reached into her coat and pulled out a switchblade. This sissy didn't know a thing about fighting, she thought. Good girls never do. She moved on Anne.

Anne backed away until she ran into the desk. She reached behind her, groping for a weapon. All she could come up with was a pen.

She held the pen in front of her, mimicking the way Brigid held the knife. "Stay back," Anne said. "I have a pen."

"What are you going to do with it, write the police chief?" Brigid shuffled forward, swiping at Anne with the knife. She was a couple of feet short. Damn eyes, she thought, and shuffled forward again.

"The pen is mightier than the sword," Anne reasoned.

"That's what people with pens say." Brigid got closer and swiped again. Anne lurched back, but Brigid sliced the pen neatly in half. "No one ever asks the people with the swords what they think." She raised the knife.

Behind Brigid, the office door flew open. Brian Skiles charged into the room, gun out. "Or the people with the guns," he said. "Drop the knife."

No chance, Brigid thought. Throw down the knife or he'll kill you.

Get him, the gang in her head ordered. Get the dumb cop bastard. It's time to do or die.

Don't listen to them, Brigid thought. They're all dead. None of them did. They all died.

But dead people don't hear voices in their heads.

Brigid spun around and threw the knife at the cop. She heard his gun go off, felt something new and hot in her body, where all had been old and dried up before.

She fell to the floor. She looked up through the cloud and saw the knife sticking into the cop's chest.

Good, she thought. I got the guy who got me. I did and I died. Then the voices in her head went out.

"Brian," Anne cried, "you're . . . you're . . ."

"No, I'm not." Brian swung open his jacket. The knife swung

away with it. "It's the notebook you gave me. I was saved by the book."

Anne knelt down by Brigid. She put her hand across Brigid's mouth, then touched the side of her neck. "She's dead."

"Tough old lady," Brian said. "Good thing I came back."

"Yes," Anne said. "But how did you figure out that Rep Gates wasn't the real killer?"

"On the way to the station, Rep kept telling me that he wasn't the killer," Brian said. "He had pretended to be the killer to scare you into buying his book. But I didn't believe him."

"Then how did you figure out that Brigid O'Hare was the real killer?"

"I didn't."

"Then why did you come back here?"

"To tell you something."

"What?"

"I love you."

Anne stood up, her eyes flaring. She faced Brian, hands fisted on her hips. "I'm in here fighting for my life, and you came back for romance?"

Anne was so angry that she didn't notice the office door open and Brandon Everall come inside carrying a manuscript. "I've got a great new book from Jill . . ." Brandon stopped suddenly when he saw the body on the floor. He looked at Brian. Then he looked at Anne and smiled when he saw how mad she was.

Anne kept yelling at Brian. "Why you self-centered, egotistical flat-head . . ."

"That's flat-foot," Brian corrected.

"Whatever you've got, I'm sure it's flat," Anne said. "I thought you were a smart cop. But it turns out you're just another love-sick jerk. What if you didn't love me? Then I'd be dead. Why, you big bum, you little . . ."

Brian never did learn what was little about him because he'd heard enough. He grabbed Anne and kissed her.

Brandon's smile faded. He moved toward them. "Don't do that," he commanded. "Don't."

They didn't pay any attention to him.

Brandon turned away in defeat. He tripped over Brigid O'Hare's body, and the manuscript flew up in the air. Three hundred pages of paper drifted down on top of Brigid O'Hare, and the last page landed across her face. The last words on the last page said:

The End

About the Author

Bob Fenster is a magazine editor, film critic and enigmatologist. When he can't spend his time solving puzzles, he likes to create them for others to solve. He has written two mysteries under a pseudonym. He lives in Northern California to show up his old New York City friends, who said he would never go far.

About the Publisher

Perseverance Press publishes a new line of old-fashioned mysteries. Emphasis is on the classic whodunit, with no excessive gore, exploitive sex, or gratuitous violence.

#1 *Death Spiral, Murder at the Winter Olympics* $8.95
by Meredith Phillips (1984)

It's a cold war on ice as love and defection breed murder at the Winter Olympics. Who killed world champion skater Dima Kuznetsov, the "playboy of the Eastern world": old or new lovers, hockey right-wingers, jealous rivals, the KGB? Will skating sleuth Lesley Grey discover the murderer before she herself is hunted down?

Reviews said: "fair-play without being easy to solve" *(Drood Review),* "timely and topical" (Allen Hubin), "surprises, suspense, and a truly unusual murder method" (Marvin Lachman), "Olympic buffs and skating fans will appreciate the frequent chats about sports-lore and Squaw Valley history" *(Kirkus Reviews).*

Not recommended for under 14 years of age.

#2 *To Prove a Villain* $8.95
by Guy M. Townsend (1985)

No one has solved this mystery in five centuries: was King Richard III responsible for the smothering of his nephews, the Little Princes, in the Tower of London?

Now, a modern-day murderer stalks a quiet college town, claiming victims in the same way. When the beautiful chairman of the English department dies, John Forest, a young history professor beset by personal and romantic problems, must grapple with both mysteries. Then he learns he may be next on the killer's list . . .

Reviews said: "a mystery set in academe that's wonderfully free from pedantry or stuffiness *(ALA Booklist),* "a tight, fast-paced tale" *(Louisville Courier-Journal),* "nicely constructed and unfailingly interesting" (Jon L. Breen), "entertaining and illuminating" (Allen Hubin).

#3 *Play Melancholy Baby* $8.95
by John Daniel (1986)

Murder most Californian: murder *in* the hot tub, murder *with* the wine bottle, murder *by* . . . ?

When the obnoxious piano player is discovered floating face down with a fractured skull, no one has a Clue whodunit. Casey has his hands full already, what with his job (playing old songs in a new world) and new and old loves, not to mention thugs of various nationalities who keep popping up.

But the past won't stay dead. When he finds himself in hot water as prime suspect and/or next victim, he realizes it's time to play Sam Spade and dig up some clues. And all he knows for sure is that it wasn't Col. Mustard.

Reviews said: "readers will thoroughly enjoy the engaging first-person narrative, snappy dialogue, and references to popular music *(ALA Booklist),* "a mellow mystery with freshly drawn characters—more Woody Allen than Clint Eastwood" (Ralph B. Sipper), "well-written and invigorating *(The Armchair Detective),* "I suggest that you 'linger awhile' with this one, for 'this is a lovely way to spend an evening' "*(Santa Barbara Magazine).*

Not recommended for under 14 years of age.

#4 *Chinese Restaurants Never Serve Breakfast* $8.95
by Roy Gilligan (1986)

The Monterey Peninsula art world is the background for private investigator Patrick Riordan's brush with death, as he stumbles across the nude, blood-covered body of a promising young painter in her Carmel cottage. On an easel nearby stands an oil painting which exactly depicts the murder scene—and which the artist has neglected to sign.

Riordan and his feisty sidekick Reiko chase clues from the galleries and boutiques of Carmel to bohemian studios in Big Sur to the moneyed world of Pebble Beach. The solution? An immutable condition, an inevitable conclusion: Chinese restaurants never serve breakfast.

Reviews said: ". . . characters are vivid and sharp . . . the narrator has an engaging, naïve charm. Gilligan also conveys the locale effectively" *(Publishers Weekly),* "a likable sleuth and writing of assured irony" (Howard Lachtman), "fast-paced, detailed and skillful—worthy of a long series" *(Monterey Herald),* "a likable work, notable for its well-realized Carmel setting, appealing characters, and unpretentiousness" *(The Armchair Detective).*

#5 *Rattlesnakes and Roses* $8.95
by Joan Oppenheimer (1987)

When Kate Regal inherits a fabulous San Diego estate, family resentment turns to murder. She must learn that being tied to the past is as futile as trying to escape from it. The bonds of love, as well as hate and jealousy, are too strong to break—a lesson which puts Kate's life in jeopardy.

Reviews said: "well-turned-out romantic suspense" (Allen Hubin), "an appealing heroine, a good story, and the perfect book for a quiet Sunday *(Union Jack),* "unexpected plot turnings and rich, concise characterization . . . Oppenheimer's natural dialogue and spare, vivid imagery make this an enjoyable, fast-moving story *(Southwest Book Review),* "well-written, cleverly constructed, and entertaining; recommended *(Small Press).*

#6 *Revolting Development* $8.95
by Lora Smith (1988)

The condo developer wasn't known for her community spirit, but that was no reason to push her out of a third-story window, or to dispose of her in a dumpster. Housewife/writer Bridget Montrose, who discovers the body, reluctantly pursues clues through Palo Alto from behind a stroller. She uncovers suburban goings-on that really belong in the dumpster, as the mystery spreads to involve friends, neighbors, and some surprisingly simpatico cops. By the time she finally tracks down the truth, the murderer's right behind her . . . .in a really revolting development.

Reviews said: "A solid whodunit" *(Ellery Queen Mystery Magazine),* "Bridget Montrose is an appealing . . . central character, and Lora Smith is a promising newcomer on the crime scene" (Jane Bakerman, *Belles Lettres,*) ". . . intelligent, believable characters and a strong plot" *(Mystery News),* ". . . an American cozy, where the plot keeps you turning the pages and the characters make you smile. Wickedly apt" *(Peninsula Times-Tribune.)*

#7 *Murder Once Done* $8.95
by Mary Lou Bennett (1988)

They came to the north Oregon coast to live out their lives in serenity, three women who'd been friends for decades. Alison's remodeled house in the quaint village of Windom was a haven for Plum and Jane. They thought they'd spend their quiet days in a little needlework, a bit of gardening, and leisurely strolls along the

beach. They thought they could forget the secret of murder once done.

But Tommy Weed, a street-smart young punk, follows them. He knows all about the murder and plans to work out his own retirement plan through blackmail. Overpowering three vulnerable old biddies ought to be a piece of cake. Age and experience are surely no match for youth and strength—or are they?

Reviews said: "Bennett knows how to turn up the suspense, and her deft blend of comedy and terror is worthy of Hitchcock in one of his chilling domestic moods" *(San Francisco Chronicle),* "The action is well staged, the characters beautifully developed" *(Ellery Queen Mystery Magazine),* ". . . delightfully refreshing, written with warmth and a perfect mix of humor and suspense" *(Mystery News),* "Well-drawn characters, a credible plot, and fine writing" (William Deeck, *The Criminal Record.*)
